DEBORAH'S SON
Rebecca Winters

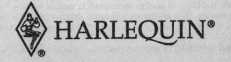

TORONTO • NEW YORK • LONDON
AMSTERDAM • PARIS • SYDNEY • HAMBURG
STOCKHOLM • ATHENS • TOKYO • MILAN • MADRID
PRAGUE • WARSAW • BUDAPEST • AUCKLAND

ISBN 0-373-70808-4

DEBORAH'S SON

Copyright © 1998 by Rebecca Winters.

This edition published by arrangement with Harlequin Books S.A.

DEBORAH'S SON

CHAPTER ONE

Mr. and Mrs. Joseph Alexander Taylor
cordially invite you
to the wedding reception
of their daughter, Rickie, and Mr. Jordan Browning
Saturday, September 10,
4:30 p.m. until 7:00 p.m. Graycliff-on-the-Hudson
Emerald Cove, New York

The bride and groom request no gifts. A donation to
the Displaced Families of New York State Charitable
Institution, administered by the Taylor Charity Begins
at Home Foundation of Poughkeepsie, New York,
would be greatly appreciated.

THE INVITATION, ENGRAVED on heavy parchment,
lay on the dashboard of the rental car. Deborah Solomon knew the words by heart. So did her brother,
David, who hadn't made a sound since they left the
Poughkeepsie airport.

Innocent in itself, the invitation to this reception
meant a fullness of joy to Rickie and her new husband, exquisite pain to David who hadn't been des-
tined to win Rickie's love. To Deborah, the invitation represented her only hope of facing Ted,
Rickie's brother, one more time.

He'd thought he'd seen the last of her after sending her a brief, heartless note four months earlier—a note telling her he'd fallen out of love with her and didn't want to see her again.

The brutal way he'd ended their relationship had killed something deep inside her. If it weren't for the news she had to tell him, she wouldn't be here now, counting the minutes until she could talk to him on his home ground. Just a few days ago, at her five-month checkup, she'd learned that the baby she was carrying was a boy. Thanks to Rickie's plan to invite her to the wedding reception without Ted's knowledge, he'd have nowhere to run from Deborah, no place to hide.

As a member of the wedding party, he would be forced to tolerate her unexpected appearance. After refusing all contact with her since sending his note, he'd left her no choice but to show up at the reception.

Of course, she'd make sure the news was for his ears alone. No matter how much he'd hurt her, she would never retaliate by embarrassing him in front of his family and friends.

Deborah's presence at the wedding of her dear friend and ally, Rickie, wasn't about revenge. Neither of the Solomons had that in mind.

The only reason David had accompanied her to New York was to lend much-needed moral support for this final confrontation. No onlooker, especially not Rickie, would know what kind of pain it cost her brother to present this show of family solidarity.

But Deborah knew.... She loved David for it. Within the hour, she would call upon his quiet strength to help her withstand the emotional ordeal awaiting her on the grounds of the Taylor estate.

"ALL RIGHT, YOU TWO. One more picture for posterity before you assemble on the lawn to greet your guests. Jordan? Stand behind your bride on the bottom step and incline your head just a little, as if you're about to kiss her.

"Rickie? Turn your head to the right to make eye contact with your husband. Lower your bouquet so it gently grazes the bottom of your chin. Edge the veil away just a trifle. That's it. Beautiful. Hold it. Perfect! Another one. Perfect!

"We're finished. Better kiss your bride, Jordan before that horde outside descends. It'll be at least three hours before your honeymoon can officially begin."

The photographer's teasing remarks sickened Ted. Amid the laughter and clapping of the wedding party, he viewed Rickie's husband with abject disgust. In fact, the very name Jordan Browning stuck in his throat like bitter gall, choking him.

For a while, the man had paraded around as Reverend Browning, part of his cover for a covert operation. He was about as religious as Ted, whose leanings toward atheism had taken a giant leap since Rickie's betrayal of him and their cousin, Bernard.

After meeting Jordan, she'd bailed out of their

plan to find their Nazi grandfather, Gerhardt von Haase, whom they believed was hiding in Paraguay.

Ted could lay that betrayal at the feet of Jordan, the ex-Navy Seal they'd hired to hunt down their monstrous relative known as the Vampire of Alsace.

Von Haase was responsible for the horrendous deaths of thousands of Jews. Ted and Bernard had vowed that if they could find him, they'd bring him to trial. His capture would be the first phase of their plan to make partial restitution to the Jewish nation for his heinous crimes against humanity.

Neither Ted nor Bernard had counted on Rickie's falling in love with Jordan. He was the one wholly responsible for the drastic change in her. His influence had caused her to call off the search and move in new directions.

Somehow, Jordan had worked on her altruistic bent to involve her in an illegal refugee airlift operation, which could result in lifetime prison sentences for both of them if they were caught.

Hell—she'd even had the audacity to ask for donations to the Displaced Families of New York State Charitable Institution in lieu of wedding presents. None of the Taylors' wealthy friends, let alone his own mother and father, had a clue that those generous wedding contributions would be supporting the repatriation, schooling, health care and placement of dozens of endangered Aché Indians illegally flown in from the Paraguayan Chaco. Rickie had done all this without batting an eye.

She glowed these days, oblivious to the inherent

dangers. Nothing bothered her. In fact, she seemed
to thrive on this precarious cause, the brainchild of
her husband and his best man, Stoney Leonard, another ex-Seal.

It didn't matter to her that Jordan had been court-
martialed and had already spent six months in prison
for killing a man against direct orders. Rickie insisted he'd risked everything to save another person's life. His actions made him a hero in her eyes.

Jordan's love had done something unfathomable
to her. Lately, Ted had even seen a new warmth
entering her relationship with their parents. He
found her reaching out to them, being more forgiv-
ing of their inability to communicate with their own
children. He understood now why they'd always
been so remote—because of the guilty secret they'd
worn year after year, like a garment. But he couldn't
forgive it. Rickie, apparently could.

As if that wasn't enough, she'd started in on Ted,
urging him to give up the idea of finding their grandfather, who might or might not still be alive. The
only thing of importance was the future, she kept
saying. She begged him to go to Deborah and tell
her the truth about von Haase. Let *her* decide if she
wanted to go on seeing the grandson of a Nazi war
criminal or not. Deborah—whose Jewish heritage
was so important to her!

For the first time in their lives, he and Rickie, who
had always been closer than most brothers and sisters, had argued. Their heated exchange had shaken
him. She'd said things to him he still resented.

"I'm going to tell you what Jordan told me," she'd announced. "You are guilty of nothing, Ted Taylor! Your only sin is the inability to forgive yourself for something that happened long before you were born and couldn't possibly have been your fault. The fact that you can't get over it thwarts your own progress, creating sin where there is none."

He shook his head now, remembering. A great sadness welled up in him as he acknowledged how far he and Rickie had grown apart, thanks to Jordan Browning.

"It's amazing what lies a man will tell himself for the sake of love," he'd responded angrily. "In a few words your fiancé has absolved you of all responsibility relating to the Holocaust, and you believe it! Let's talk a little honesty here. He wanted you for himself and was willing to say anything to have you."

"You're wrong, Ted. One day when it's too late, you'll know just how wrong. None of us can change the past, but if you don't let go of your guilt, you'll destroy Deborah as surely as our parents' guilty secret estranged our family.

"Think what you're doing! Are you really any different than Mother or Father if you shut Deborah out with no explanation, no consideration for her feelings?"

Her inability to understand appalled him. "Has love for Jordan Browning made you deaf, dumb and blind to the pain our family secret would inflict on the Solomons, of all people?"

Rickie had changed beyond recognition, or she wouldn't have suggested he reveal the truth. Ted could never have handled Deborah's shock, let alone her horror, and her family's revulsion.

They had embraced him like a son, something his own parents had never been able to do.

The only solution had been to end their relationship with a simple lie. Every day, lovers around the world broke up because one of the partners had lost interest. Deborah would have to accept his explanation. She was young; eventually she would recover from his rejection. In any event, the matter was closed and had been for some time now.

It seemed Bernard was the only person left who shared Ted's burden and understood.

A feeling of isolation swept over him as he watched his sister respond to another of Jordan's passionate embraces before they went outside to greet the wedding guests. She belonged to her husband now.

You've abandoned me, Rickie.

I need another drink fast.

To his relief, Bernard had preceded him to the study. For the moment, he and his cousin were alone.

"I have one ready for you," the ever-loyal Bernard muttered, extending Ted a Scotch while he nursed his own drink. "These tuxes are going to be hell in the heat. Who would have guessed September would be this hot?"

Ted groaned an acknowledgment, then finished

off his drink in a couple of swallows. "Rickie insisted on an outdoor wedding. I can't say I blame her. This place is nothing more than a pretentious mausoleum. The upkeep alone could fund her latest project indefinitely." Having delivered his acid remark, he poured himself another Scotch.

"Except that she wouldn't touch the money from it." Bernard rested his empty glass on the bar's counter. "I think maybe we'd better head outside before someone comes looking for us."

"I don't particularly care if we're missed or not. There's something important I need to talk over with you first," he explained, lowering his voice in case anyone came into the study.

"If it's about Stoney leading us to von Haase, I'm way ahead of you. Unfortunately, he and Jordan are like this." He held up two crossed fingers.

"Not Stoney." Ted flashed his cousin a shrewd glance. "Father DeSilva."

The mention of the priest who'd helped officiate at Rickie's wedding ceremony produced a frown from Bernard. "I thought of approaching him, but his loyalties are with Jordan and Stoney."

"For their airlift operation, yes. But the priest has no idea Jordan had another agenda when he flew down to the Chaco—that time Rickie hid on board."

"You mean Father DeSilva didn't know they were looking for our grandfather?"

"No."

"How can you be so sure?"

"Rickie told me." After a brief silence, "One thing I'll say for her. She has never lied to me."

"Nor me."

"When she called off the search, she made it clear that no one knew our secret yet, and that was the way she wanted it to stay. I promised her I wouldn't approach Jordan again, but I never promised to stop looking for von Haase."

"Ted...something tells me the only way we'd ever get that man's attention would be to tell him the truth. And once we did, he'd never cooperate. Helping us hunt for our grandfather would put his life in even greater jeopardy."

"According to Rickie, he's a hunted man who escaped from prison. His days are numbered for supposed crimes against the dictatorship. He runs an underground for political prisoners, which means he risks his life every single day. To my way of thinking, he's the perfect person to approach."

"Even if that's true, we don't have much time. Stoney's flying him back to the Chaco day after tomorrow."

"I've got a plan. I'll tell you about it on the way outside. Let's be thankful Rickie and Jordan will be leaving for Tahiti tomorrow."

"How long are they going to be gone?"

"I'm not sure. I heard Rickie say something about a couple of weeks, but then Jordan laughed and said a month, at least. If that's the case, we ought to be able to accomplish our objective before their return."

"Rickie will find out."

"That's no longer my concern. I don't have a sister anymore, Bernard."

"You don't mean that!"

"The hell I don't." He poured himself a third glass. "She's chosen the side she's on. It's not ours."

"I think the Glenmorangie '71 is doing most of the talking." Bernard took the glass from him. "Come on, Ted. I've never seen you drink like this before. Look, I know the real reason you're in so much pain right now. But this is Rickie's big day. Don't spoil it for her."

Ted eyed his cousin grimly, but what was left of his conscience chose not to argue with him. Together they left the study through the nearest set of French doors and stepped onto the sheltered patio.

After the air-conditioning inside, the combination of heat and humidity this close to the river stifled him. It brought back unpleasant childhood memories he'd just as soon forget, memories of an unsatisfactory relationship with parents who were never around during the long summer months when school was out, who never allowed their children to know them. Ted and Rickie had clung to each other for survival.

Chamber music, mixed with the sounds of people's happy voices, drifted up from the grounds, reminding him that Rickie had someone else to turn to now. Her marriage had changed their whole lives.

His growing sense of isolation increased his dread of the long night still to come.

"If nothing else," Bernard murmured as they crossed the expanse of velvety green lawn, "you owe Rickie for not telling Deborah the truth behind your back. It just about killed Rickie when you told her she couldn't ask Deborah to be a bridesmaid. Those two were close. She thought she was getting a sister-in-law."

"Tell me about it. Deborah was my life."

"I know that," came the other man's grave response.

"When I cut her off, I felt something inside me die."

"I know that, too."

"I don't want to talk about her. We've got our work cut out. We have to engage Father DeSilva's help without anyone else being aware of it. Whichever one of us gets to him before the reception is over has to find out his agenda for tomorrow."

"THAT'S ODD. We just passed the sign for Emerald Cove, but I don't see a town anywhere."

"There isn't one. Rickie said to take the turnoff two miles ahead. It leads to their estate," replied Deborah.

"How come Ted never brought you out here to meet his parents?" In the next instant David reached over to squeeze her hand. "I'm sorry. I should have kept my mouth shut."

"Don't apologize. I asked myself that question

every time I flew into Poughkeepsie to be with him, but his mother and father were the one subject he refused to discuss.''

David let out a sigh. ''Rickie wasn't quite as reticent. She intimated that they'd always felt estranged from their parents, but I could tell she didn't like talking about them, either.''

Deborah stared out the window, barely noticing the scenery. ''She promised me that one day after we were married, Ted would break down and tell me everything going on inside him...because he loved me.''

There was a time, centuries ago, before Ted had broken off with her, when Deborah had believed that.

Though they lived on different continents, she and Ted had been virtually inseparable from their first meeting at the Solomon home in Jerusalem six and a half months earlier.

He'd been on vacation in Egypt and Israel with his sister, who'd met David in Australia. Because of that friendship, the Solomons had invited them to visit when they got to Jerusalem. Ted and Rickie happened to be talking to her parents in their living room when Deborah rushed in.

This was her first leave from the army in several months. She'd jumped down from the back of the truck that had dropped her off in front of the house. Then she'd hurried inside to surprise her parents, not realizing until too late that they had company.

Jerusalem swarmed with thousands of tourists

every year. Her gregarious parents, who worked at the Holocaust memorial ushering English-speaking visitors around, often entertained guests in their home.

Her father's family had come to Jerusalem from Ukraine, and earlier in his life he'd spent several years in England, attending school.

Her mother's family had moved from Kiev to Denmark, where the children in their Jewish neighborhood had been privately tutored by an English professor living in Copenhagen at the time. Their education had been interrupted when they'd had to flee the Nazis.

From the time Deborah and David were little children, their parents had insisted that English be an essential part of their education. Therefore, the sight of her parents chatting comfortably with two Americans wasn't at all unusual.

For the most part, Deborah didn't particularly care for Americans. Their open friendliness always seemed a trifle suspect to her, if not insincere. Their conversation generally revealed inadequate schooling on international affairs, and little comprehension of Israel or its people.

They weren't unintelligent—just uninformed. As far as Deborah was concerned, their worst fault lay in their indifference. They didn't seem to worry that they knew or understood so little about the world or anything that didn't directly concern them.

But all of those uncharitable thoughts she shelved in deference to her brother, who'd fallen in love with

Rickie Taylor. His letters from Australia were full of praise and admiration for the wealthy young philanthropist whose sweetness had wound its way into his heart.

That fact alone forced Deborah to summon a more tolerant attitude toward their guests. These two people, with their classic bone structure and fair coloring, were among the most attractive she'd ever met.

Something that set them apart was their ash-blond hair of so fine a shade and texture it gleamed a silvery-gold even though the living room had been darkened by shutters.

Having been born and raised among dark-haired, dark-eyed people, Deborah found her gaze returning again and again to their visitors after they'd been introduced. No wonder David had been enamored of Rickie's charms from the outset. She was lovely in that blond, northern European way.

Rickie's brother, who appeared to be around thirty, was equally beautiful according to masculine standards. Deborah knew it was rude to stare, but she couldn't help it. Ted Taylor had no physical flaws she could see.

Words like *good-looking* or *handsome* failed to describe him. It wasn't just his six-foot-two-inch height and powerful build or the fact that he looked both elegant and masculine in a lightweight white sport shirt and gabardine trousers.

When he spoke, she noted an intelligence in his dark blue eyes. He displayed a certain sensitivity on any number of difficult subjects, revealing a depth of character she hadn't run across in most of her male acquaintances over the last twenty-six years, be they Jew or Gentile.

On top of everything else, there was an intangible aura of authority about him, a built-in confidence as he discussed topics initiated by her parents. The sophisticated ease with which he conversed, plus his grasp of the political ideologies and current issues affecting Israel, intrigued and impressed the family. But no one was more impressed than Deborah.

Within a few minutes of meeting him, he became larger than life to her. Throughout the rest of that afternoon, without any volition on her part, her mind and heart opened up to receive him. All of him.

By the time the five of them had sat down together for the evening meal, she realized that, like her brother, she also had been caught off guard by the Taylor charisma.

She should have gone to bed when everyone else retired. Instead, she'd been flattered by his invitation to stay up and tell him about her life, particularly her duties in the army.

She didn't quite know how it happened, but they talked quietly until after three in the morning. Embarrassed because she'd all but bared her soul to him, Deborah forced herself to say good-night. Before he let her go, he extracted a promise that the next day she'd show him the Jerusalem she cherished.

Unable to quell her pounding heart, she'd gone to bed, but sleep didn't come easily that night or on any of the subsequent nights of her leave. They'd fallen in love and didn't want to waste a second of their precious time together during those idyllic weeks.

Before work and duty tore them apart, Ted proposed marriage and she accepted. They decided that once they were husband and wife, they would live in New York but commute to Jerusalem as often as possible. He would buy an apartment there, close to her family.

After presenting their plan, they obtained her parents' blessing, a feat Deborah considered nothing short of miraculous.

There was a discussion of her resignation from the army, the logistics of planning their marriage.

The next time she was in New York she'd planned to search for a rabbi who'd be willing to perform the ceremony for her and her non-Jewish fiancé. But no matter the obstacles or ramifications of Torah law, she had refused to let anything interfere with their happiness.

Ted loved her in the same soul-searching way she loved him; she was sure that a love like theirs rarely came along in this lifetime. She realized she was one of the lucky ones and thanked God for such a great blessing.

Then there'd been that cruel and inexplicable note....

What went wrong?

"QUICK— Deborah, take a look at that!"

The wonder in David's voice roused her from despair long enough to glance in the direction he was pointing. She let out a faint gasp.

They'd grown up there? In that version of Sleeping Beauty's castle?

David's whistle expressed her own unspoken thoughts. "Once when I asked Rickie about her home, she told me their family estate had been featured in a documentary about America's castles. At the time I laughed, not understanding. What a fool I was," he said, his voice shaking, "about everything."

"I was a worse fool, David," she told him bitterly. The reality of Ted's birthright had ripped the veil from her eyes.

"I believed the attractive American man who stands next in line to run the world's most powerful banking corporation—the man whose ancestors were English aristocracy—actually wanted to marry *me*, an insignificant woman whose relatives were pretty much annihilated by the Nazis.

"I can boast of nothing more than a university diploma on my bedroom wall and a semiautomatic machine gun at my side.

"I guess ours was a case of opposites attracting. But after the initial excitement faded, he reconsidered his options and backed out." She gave a shrug that was meant to seem indifferent, resigned.

"Don't!"

"Don't what? Face the truth? There's the truth in

all its glory staring straight at us. I don't know why I didn't recognize any of this sooner.

"It doesn't take great intelligence to understand that I provided an interesting distraction during an otherwise dull vacation. By being available at any hour, day or night, I played right into his hands until he grew bored of us. My naiveté must have come as such a shock, it was the only reason he kept up the pretense as long as h—"

"For heaven's sake, Deborah! He really did some damage, didn't he?"

You have no idea, David.

She stirred restlessly. "I'm frightened."

He looked over at her with compassionate brown eyes. "You think I don't know that? But I refuse to let you talk about yourself this way. Don't demean yourself or the love you felt for him. This behavior isn't worthy of you. *He* isn't worthy of you. You're going to say what you have to say to Ted, then we're going to give Rickie our best wishes and leave."

"He might see me first and run."

"If he's too cowardly to hear you out, then you'll know your worst assessment of him was right. Whatever happens, after tonight you're going to put all this away for good."

I wish I could, David. I wish it were that simple.

CHAPTER TWO

"NICE TO SEE YOU AGAIN, Senator." The two men shook hands.

"Good to see you again, my boy. You've been a difficult person to get hold of lately. It must be all the wedding fuss, eh? Rickie's a beautiful bride. How does it feel to have a new brother-in-law join the lofty Taylor ranks?"

Ted fought to keep his composure in front of John Mason, one of the senators from New York, a man close to the president and someone Ted genuinely respected. No doubt he'd come to convey his congratulations to Rickie and discuss a little business at the same time.

"The fact that Rickie's marrying him is a good enough endorsement for me."

The lies kept compounding. All their lives were a lie. Rickie's, Bernard's, their parents'—

The older man inclined his head. "Speaking of endorsements..." he murmured in a confiding tone. "Next week I'm having lunch with some people, including Arthur Middleton, a possible candidate for a position on the Federal Reserve Board. It would mean a great deal if you could join us, feel him out. I'd like your assessment and input to take to the president. He values your opinion. It won't be long before he'll present your name for an appointment.''

That was the last thing Ted wanted. As for Middleton, he had conservative leanings that would make him a safe choice to fill the appointment. With John's backing, Middleton had a good chance of winning the Senate's approval.

''I'm honored that you would ask for my opinion, and I'd be happy to oblige. But I'm afraid I'll be out of town for the next couple of weeks.'' He hoped those were prophetic words.

John's eyes twinkled. ''Business or pleasure?''

A picture of von Haase helpless before his accusers rose in Ted's mind. ''Pleasure...most definitely.''

''Does that mean there's going to be another wedding in the Taylor family soon?''

The perfectly natural question hit Ted like an unexpected knockout blow. Like water bursting through a dam, memories of Deborah as he'd last seen her came flooding back. Memories accompanied by guilt.

The other man clapped him on the shoulder. ''Forgive me for the question. Next time just tell me to mind my own business.''

In spite of his pain, Ted warmed to John, whose apology couldn't be construed as anything but sincere. He flashed him a quick smile.

''Tonight everyone's asked me the same question. It's Rickie's last act of revenge against her bachelor brother for former grievances. Sticking me in this clown suit was just the beginning.''

John's head reared back in laughter. When the laughter subsided he said more quietly, ''I'll put that meeting on hold until you return.''

There seemed to be no chance of getting out of it. ''All right. Ask your secretary to set up a date and time with mine.''

''Splendid, my boy.''

As he moved on to shake hands with one of Rickie's bridesmaids, Bernard muttered, ''Don't look now, but Father DeSilva just signed the guest book and is headed our way.''

''Good. That'll save us the trouble of hunting him down later on. Is he alone?''

''No. Reverend Rolon's right behind him.''

''Since he and Jordan are such close friends, we're going to have to be careful not to say anything that could get back to Jordan about our plans.''

''Father.'' He heard Bernard greet the priest. ''Between you and Reverend Rolon, it was a wonderful ceremony. I was very moved.''

''So was I, Father,'' Ted interjected, grasping the wiry priest's hands.

''The privilege was all ours, was it not, Reverend?'' He deferred to the other clergyman who nodded his assent.

''Now that your official duties are over,'' Bernard continued, ''we hope you'll be able to enjoy some of New York's sights before your return to Paraguay.''

"I had that pleasure yesterday, Mr. Taylor."

Ted's mouth curved upward in amusement. "I hardly think one day is enough, Father."

"I'm afraid it's all the time I can afford."

"When are you going back?"

"The day after tomorrow."

"Then you'll have to make the most of the short time you have left."

He nodded. "I plan to. Tomorrow I'm lunching with the pastor of St. Catherine's Church in Poughkeepsie."

Ted didn't need to make eye contact with Bernard to know that Reverend Rolon's New York underground involved churches other than his own.

The need to help the Hispanic community was so critical, the leaders of many different faiths often came together to solve problems. And one of those problems was interference from the long arm of the law.

No doubt the reverend had set up this seemingly innocent lunch for Father DeSilva in an effort to establish new contacts for their covert activities.

"It sounds like you're taking what we call a busman's holiday," Bernard teased.

Father DeSilva smiled. "I know that expression. You are right. I'm afraid that when you get to be my age, you become a creature of habit. I do better in familiar surroundings."

"Then we hope your visit with the pastor will be a pleasant one. Thanks again for making Rickie and Jordan's wedding day so perfect. It meant a lot to them that you'd come such a long way to perform the ceremony.''

Piercing black eyes bore into Ted's. ''Your sister is a very special soul in the sight of God. So is Jordan. I'm the one who is honored.''

Ted stared back, disturbed because Rickie had changed in such bewildering ways. Something told him this priest had a certain amount of influence over her. Ted didn't like it, but there wasn't much he could do. In fact, it was shamefully hypocritical of him to feel like this when he and Bernard were about to ask Father DeSilva for his help.

DEBORAH SPOTTED Ted from a long way off. In any crowd he'd be impossible to miss. The last rays of the sun disappearing below the horizon gilded his hair, giving it a metallic sheen.

That fateful afternoon when her parents had first introduced her to Ted Taylor, she'd been captivated by everything about him. From that day on, her world had changed and it would never be the same again. As for Ted, he'd enjoyed her company for a time, but had since moved on. He'd put it bluntly enough in his letter: he didn't love her anymore.

He couldn't have seen her yet, not poised as she was behind David. Ted had never met him, since David had been in Australia for the past year finishing up his doctorate. In fact, he'd only seen pictures of her brother, although David hadn't been wearing his glasses in any of them. Today he'd worn them and looked older, more sophisticated.

The humid heat had grown unbearable. Her loose-fitting silk dress clung to her body, made moist by perspiration. With the two of them sandwiched between other wilting guests, she fairly gasped for breath. It made her wonder how the bridesmaids could still look so fresh.

If it hadn't been for Ted's betrayal of their love, Deborah would have been standing there next to Rickie.

The bridesmaids were lovely, draped in feminine pale yellow chiffon that fell to midcalf. In their arms they carried sheaves of long-stemmed yellow roses. The same roses lay in clusters above their dreamy, broad-brimmed hats.

In contrast, the fairy-tale bridal couple were in traditional black and white. They stood on the perfect green lawns against the backdrop of a French Renaissance garden. With every element in place, this had to be the storybook wedding of the decade.

Deborah's heart went out to her brother, who couldn't take his eyes off the bride. Poor David, with his gentleness and unremarkable looks. His pure love and innocent devotion for Rickie caused him to exist in a dream state.

Deborah hoped Rickie's marriage to Jordan would wake David up to reality. Until he could admit that she'd never been his to begin with, her brother would never get over her. Never go on to the next stage in his life.

Rickie Taylor, now Rickie Browning, had beauty of soul as well as body. Deborah understood David's dilemma. It would be no use comparing Rickie to other women, because there *was* no comparison. Her brother would have to make the effort to meet someone entirely different....

What worried Deborah was that it might be a long while before that happened.

The line moved forward, and she came closer to the moment when Ted would be forced to face her one final time. "We're almost there," David whispered out of the side of his mouth.

She grabbed hold of his arm and clung to him. "Do you think he's seen me yet?"

"Of course not. He's too besieged by guests. There must be several thousand people here. I've never seen anything like it."

With every step, her pulse rate accelerated. Angry at herself because she'd wanted to present a calm, cool facade to the man who'd rejected her, she tried taking a deep breath to gain some vestige of control.

"Deborah? Are you all right? Your face is flushed."

"It's just the heat." In truth, she was running a slight temperature. Because of the anxiety? The uncertainty?

Rickie had convinced her their plan would work. But all their talk had been pure theory. Deborah hadn't realized she'd feel so...ill, with this weakness attacking her limbs or the unnatural beating of her heart.

In an effort to keep out of sight, she sheltered closer to her brother who was Ted's height and a good eight inches taller than she was. "How many people between us and him?"

"Three."

Dear God.

"If this is too painful, we can leave the reception right now."

"No. I have to follow through with this."

"Then brace yourself. I know what to do."

Already she could pick out Bernard Taylor's voice from among a myriad of others.

Deborah was crazy about Ted's cousin. The two men were closer than most brothers. When Ted had called off their engagement, he'd destroyed so much that had brought her joy, including her growing friendship with Bernard.

Another couple of steps now, and she heard her brother introducing himself to Ted's cousin. That was her signal to move. With the blood pounding in her ears, she slipped past them.

An elegantly dressed older woman and her husband still held Ted's attention as Deborah came to a standstill in front of the man she would always love.

The instant before he became aware of her presence, her hungry gaze took inventory of his face. She detected shadows beneath his eyes and a faint flush on his skin, which was pulled taut over his cheekbones. He was leaner than she'd ever seen him, and his features had a chiseled look. By the looser fit of his black tuxedo, she could tell he'd lost weight.

Suddenly his head turned in her direction. In that second before his body went rigid and his eyes narrowed, she glimpsed unspeakable pain in those frozen blue depths, as if he carried the weight of the world on his shoulders.

He had suffered.

Why?

All these weeks, so many violent emotions had been vying for supremacy, Deborah thought she'd explode from the tumult. Yet overriding her pent-up rage was this totally unexpected welling of compassion for him.

Stepping close enough to smell the alcohol on his breath, she said quietly, "I didn't come to the wedding to ask you for anything. Only to tell you something. You're going to be a father at the end of December. One day when our son is old enough to ask the most important question of his life, he will have expected this much from me. Shalom, Ted."

On the verge of collapse, Deborah was grateful for her brother, who knew she wanted nothing more than to vanish from sight.

Their flight toward the small army of young men providing valet parking for the guests seemed hazy. At one point her feet didn't even touch the ground. Without David's help, she would have collapsed on the grass and made the spectacle she'd prayed to avoid.

Not until they were speeding their way to Poughkeepsie did she begin to have any sort of awareness of her surroundings.

"Before I die, I'm going to make damn certain that blue-eyed bastard rots in hell for rejecting you."

No, David.

"THIS IS QUITE an affair, Ted. Judging by all the photographers and reporters, it'll make every major newspaper."

A son?

"We haven't seen you at the club lately. Hear you've been spending a lot of time overseas."

Deborah was going to bear his son in December?

"I was hoping we could get together for a meeting with the stockholders in the next few days. We'll set a time at your convenience."

What have I done?

"You wouldn't remember me. I was friends with your parents before I moved to the West Coast in the seventies."

I've defiled her.

"You and Rickie are so grown-up, I don't recognize you anymore. It doesn't seem very long ago that the two of you were racing around here playing one crazy game or other."

If she knew she were carrying a von Haase in her womb, it would kill her.

"This is a beautiful reception, Ted. I told your father as much. Speaking of your dad, see if you can't talk him into that Midwest bank merger we were discussing the other day. It makes good business sense all the way around."

I've got to get out of here.

"Finally! Do you know how long I've been waiting in line? There ought to be a law. Listen, I have something important to tell you two. I couldn't say anything at the office."

I'm going to be sick.

"Hey, Ted? Where are you going? Bernard? Where's he going?"

"He needed a break. Relax. It's almost time for the bride and groom to cut the cake. You can talk to him then."

"TED?"

The tapping on the bathroom door grew louder.

"Are you all right?"

Ted's clammy hands gripped the top of the tank while he vomited for the sixth time. He hadn't had anything but Scotch in the last twelve hours.

"For God's sake, let me in so I can help you!"

I don't want help, Bernard. I want oblivion.

He rested his forehead against the cool tile and waited to see if there was going to be another episode.

"A few minutes ago you looked like death, and I know why. I heard her, Ted. I'm sure Deborah didn't want me to, but I did."

Ted used his foot to shove the tux jacket and tie out of his way. He'd ripped them off when he'd first run into the bathroom. Still unsteady, he moved to the sink and rinsed his mouth.

"You think I don't know what Deborah's news has done to you? Talk to me!"

Months ago, he and Bernard had learned the definition of hell when they'd traveled to Metz, France, and been presented with proof of their true lineage as von Haases.

But Bernard hadn't loved Deborah—hadn't defiled her. Hadn't made her pregnant. *With another von Haase.*

This thought had opened a whole new cavern of pain inside Ted.

Great heaving sobs shook his body. Slowly he sank to the edge of the tub, then the floor.

"Ted—"

Ted heard alarm and love in his cousin's outcry but couldn't answer him.

"Ted! If you don't come out of there soon, Rickie'll realize something's wrong. They're cutting the wedding cake right now. I'm sure she's noticed you're not around—she's probably sick with worry."

Rickie wasn't sick with worry; he was positive of that. She'd known exactly what she was doing when she'd invited the Solomons to the reception. Knowing Deborah's condition, Rickie had one more card left, and she'd played it.

"Don't do this, Ted, or you'll live to regret it. She's your sister. She loves you. Don't ruin her wedding day. It's almost over. She'll be gone soon. Come on. I'm here for you."

"Were you in on it, too, Bernard?" he lashed out, although he knew the truth. Bernard would never betray him.

"I'm going to give you two minutes to pull yourself together. If you're not out of there by then, I'm breaking down the door. The decision is yours."

"Don't bother, Bernard." A second voice floated from the other side of the door. Rickie's!

Ted felt a fresh stab of pain.

"I only have a few minutes before Jordan wonders where I am. I'm not going to apologize for my actions. When you broke off with Deborah, you refused to give her a chance to tell you about the baby. She *loves* you, Ted, and she wanted to tell you to your face.

"So I did the only thing I could. What you choose to do with that knowledge is your business.

"The Ted I used to know was a man of great honor. Think about it this way. Perhaps that baby does carries the von Haase genes. But he also carries the genes of von Haase's victims.

"Are you willing to make your own son another von Haase victim?"

Shut up, Rickie.

"The Ted I grew up with wouldn't dream of leaving his own son without a father. The Ted I've idolized from childhood wouldn't be capable of forcing the mother of his son into another man's arms to help her raise *his* child."

Stop!

"Doesn't it bother you just a little bit that, in time, Deborah will find a substitute to act as your son's father? She's a beautiful woman, inside and out. You fell in love with her. Other men have, too. I've seen their reactions around her. So have you.

"The truth is, any man would want her and thank God to have her. Whoever that man is, he'll be willing to raise your son."

For the love of God, don't say any more!

"Is that what you want? Someone else doing the job only you were meant to do?"

There was a moment's silence, then Rickie went relentlessly on. "Maybe the picture is more pleasant visualizing her raising your son alone. Can you see Deborah as a single mom, struggling to be both mother and father?

"The Solomons make an adequate living, but their home is small, and you and I know another child will put a strain on their finances. Knowing Deborah's pride, I can hardly see her relying on them. When I offered my help, she turned me down flat."

If you don't stop talking—

"You're aware how difficult it'll be to find a good apartment in a nice part of Jerusalem, one that doesn't cost a fortune. She'll have to live more frugally than before. But once she's had the baby, I understand she can still be in the army and keep her child at a day care center.

"Or there's the possibility that if she chooses to use her university degree, she won't be able to find a good teaching position for several years. That'll force her to take an entry-level job of some kind. It won't pay enough to give her the decent housing she'll require for her and the baby.

"But what can she expect when her lover claims no responsibility for the baby they created together? Think about it, Ted!"

Lord, Rickie.

The tears dripped off his chin. He reached for a towel to dry them. Never in his wildest dreams could he have imagined his sister speaking to him like this. Her speech brought him to his feet, just as it was calculated to do. He would have opened the door, but he was too weak and fell against it instead.

"Rickie?"

There was an ominous silence.

"Rickie!" he cried.

"She's gone, Ted. The bouquet's been thrown. Everybody's outside in the drive, waiting to shower them with rice."

"For my sake, go wave her off."

"For your sake, I'm not budging. You need me. She doesn't."

Bernard spoke the truth. Now that Rickie had Jordan, her world was complete.

"When you're ready, come on out and we'll talk about someone who needs you—and only you—quite desperately."

Ted had no idea how much time had passed before he picked up his clothes and opened the door. His cousin eyed his disheveled state with grave concern.

"You look like hell."

They gave each other a frank stare.

Ted finally shook his head. "How could she have gotten pregnant? I always took precautions." An exasperated sigh escaped. "No. Don't answer that."

"I won't."

"Do you want to know something ironic? I told Deborah I'd be willing to wait until our wedding night before I made love to her for the first time. But she didn't want to wait."

He raised his eyes to the ceiling, fighting more tears.

"She said her life in the army made her realize just how precious every minute was, that it could be snatched away with one terrorist bomb, one single bullet.

"She'd never had a lover. She'd been saving herself for the man she wanted to marry. She told me I was that man. She begged me to make love to her, just in case something terrible happened and we never saw each other again.

"After we made love the first time, we couldn't stop. That's why we moved up the wedding date. I asked her to get out of the army. I wanted her to live in Poughkeepsie with me. I promised to keep her safe, to give her a long, happy life. I promised her children."

More deep-seated sobs shook his body.

"At least you kept your last promise," Bernard reminded him. "I don't see what's to prevent you from keeping the rest. Marriage to Deborah doesn't have to interfere with our plans to track down von Haase.''

What?

''Just think, Ted—if we find him and turn him over to the Jewish authorities for trial, don't you imagine she and her family could find a way to forgive you for being his grandson?''

Since learning that his grandfather's last name was von Haase, not Taylor, nothing in Ted's life had made sense, not until this moment.

If they could find their grandfather, would it be enough to erase Deborah's loathing?

''Of course,'' Bernard continued in the same vein, ''getting her to marry you now, after so much damage has been done, might require a bit of cunning.

''So far you've been a formidable adversary. I suspect that facing you this evening took more courage than confronting any dangerous situation she's run across as a soldier. In my opinion, her bravery deserves a medal. Yet you let her walk away.''

I know that, Bernard. Don't you realize it's killing me?

''She's not going to forgive that easily. You'll have to come up with one hell of a good reason for cutting things off with her the way you did. In fact, I have a feeling that if you decide to go after her, you're in for some emotional trauma of a different sort.''

Tell me something I don't know.

''Why don't we pay a little visit to St. Catherine's

Church tomorrow? If the priest isn't willing to help us, we'll find someone else who is.

"But if he agrees to cooperate, let's at least find out what kind of time frame we're working with here. It only makes sense that the sooner you get married, the sooner we can take off for Paraguay without distractions. And here's the beauty of it all.

"If for some reason something should happen to you, Deborah will have the Taylor name. She'll be set for life. So will your son. As for your secret, it'll stay buried with you. That can be your legacy. Think about it while I get changed out of this monkey suit."

I'm thinking, Bernard.

CHAPTER THREE

"DEBORAH? I'm sorry I've been so impossible. Do you feel like talking?"

Even though they'd attained cruising speed, the Fasten Seat Belt sign stayed on. Some of the passengers disregarded it, but Deborah had to think of the tiny life growing inside her. If the plane should meet with turbulence, she wanted to be protected.

"What is there to say, David? Rickie was so sure Ted would break down when he saw me. But he didn't say one word to me, let alone ask me to stay until after the reception so we could talk. And that convinces me he never had any real feeling for me in the first place.

"It was just a strong sexual attraction. Temporary madness happens to millions of people every year. Lots of women end up with babies to raise alone. I'm just another statistic.

"After visiting Graycliff, I have a better understanding of Ted. A man of his background—already born to so much wealth—doesn't want the normal kind of life you and I cherish. It simply wouldn't be enough to hold him. He has to be constantly on the move, seeking new thrills to keep his charmed life from becoming monotonous.

"Last evening I glimpsed a bleakness in his eyes. They didn't light up when he saw me. My presence scarcely registered with him. Whatever fleeting attraction he once felt, it's dead.

"But I'm not sorry I went to the reception. I've done my duty for my unborn son. One day when he asks me about his daddy, I can tell him the truth, that his biological father is a man to be pitied."

David turned his head toward her. "If that's true, then how do you explain Rickie? She comes from the same background, but she's not anything like her brother."

"I'm not so sure about that."

"What do you mean?" he demanded with uncharacteristic sharpness, and sat up straighter. He didn't like the idea that Rickie could be anything less than perfect. Maybe it was time to raise a question or two in David's mind about her suitability for him.

"Since I trust you with my life and I know you can keep a secret, I'm going to tell you a few facts about Rickie. Don't get me wrong. I love her. But she's not who you think she is. For one thing, when Rickie returned from Australia and met Jordan for the first time, he'd just been released from prison for killing a man."

David's eyes rounded in astonishment. "What?"

From the sudden pallor of her brother's complexion, she realized she'd really shocked him. Good. He needed a strong jolt if he was ever to get past Rickie and move on to someone else.

After giving him a detailed explanation of Rickie and Jordan's daring covert operation in the Chaco, she pulled the wedding invitation from her purse. "Do you see where it asks for donations to that charity in lieu of wedding gifts?"

"Good Lord. You mean—"

"I do mean. One day she and Jordan could be in a lot of trouble from the authorities for their illegal airlifts. Rickie enjoys living dangerously. For a girl who's had literally everything handed to her all her life, including great health and beauty, what else is there?

"Now that you know a few truths, you should be able to understand why you were never in the running."

His jaw hardened. In toppling Rickie from her pedestal, Deborah had made him suffer. It pained her to be this honest, but someone had to remove the blinders.

"Maybe now you're beginning to see a pattern in brother *and* sister? They come from a dysfunctional family." She drove the point home. "It's not like ours where there's an abundance of love. We're the lucky ones, David."

"You're right about that."

After clearing his throat he didn't say anything else, which was a good sign. It meant he was listening at last.

"Let's be honest," Deborah said quietly. "The kind of quiet, steady home life with two or three children that you and I envision for ourselves doesn't quite fulfill the Taylors' expectations.''

"I must have been out of my mind.'' She detected resignation in his voice. Good.

"If it makes you feel any better, we both were. I'll admit it was exciting while it lasted." Tears stung her eyes but she willed them not to fall. She'd done enough crying before she'd left for New York.

"The Taylors are probably the most unique, remarkable, beautiful people we'll ever meet in our lifetime. Our one brush with America's royalty. Something to talk about in our old age."

After an extended silence, David asked, "What are you going to tell my nephew about Ted?"

"That's right." She squeezed his arm. "He *will* be your nephew. Well, I've made up my mind about one thing. I'm not going to say a word until he asks."

"Your son probably won't be able to believe it when you finally do tell him about his Taylor heritage."

"I can only hope that by then he'll be all grown-up, with a strong, abiding love of the Solomon family—and an understanding of our values."

"Deborah? As soon as we get back, why don't we get an apartment together? At least for a while. I've been living on my own in Australia for so long, I'd like the company. But I don't feel right about living at home anymore."

"That's a wonderful idea! I feel exactly the same way. In fact, I was planning to go apartment-hunting tomorrow. If I can move in with you, Mom and Dad won't give me such a hard time about it. Now that I'm expecting, you'd think I was an invalid.''

"Try hearing every day that it's time I did the right thing and got married. They had a wife picked out for me by my bar mitzvah. Remember Rebecca Finklestein?''

Deborah nodded. "She's still single. I know a secret, but you can't tell Mom and Dad.''

"What is it?''

"Both sets of parents are still hoping.''

"That's a secret?''

"You're right. Nothing's new.'' She paused. "That thought's rather comforting, don't you think?''

For the first time in months they could both smile about something.

It's a start, Deborah.

You want David to move on? Then don't be a hypocrite.

Keep smiling and forget that Ted has shattered every dream.

"YOU WANT ME to hear your confessions? That's the reason you've been following me? Rickie didn't tell me the two of you had converted to Catholicism.''

The shrewd priest exhibited a surprising sense of humor Ted couldn't help admiring.

He made eye contact with his cousin as they accompanied Father DeSilva from the rectory where he'd been in conference with the pastor for the last two hours.

"If we could talk privately, Father...?"

The older priest slowed his steps. "I was about to take a taxi back to my hotel."

"Allow us to drive you there," Bernard offered. "Our car's out front. Your time is limited, I know, but what we have to say won't take long."

"I must admit I'm intrigued," came the comment as Ted helped him into the back seat of the Mercedes. Father DeSilva told them which hotel he was staying at, and they were off.

Ted positioned himself in the corner of the back seat, where he could observe the priest's reactions. "Father? Have you ever heard of the Nazi war criminal Gerhardt von Haase?"

He nodded. "Who hasn't? His atrocities are legion. I understand he was never caught." He eyed Ted directly. "Of what interest is von Haase to you?"

They were stopped at a light. Bernard looked over his shoulder at the priest. "He's our grandfather."

The priest sat there, making no movement or sound.

"Less than six months ago, we didn't know of his existence," Ted continued. "Our parents made up the name Taylor and to cover their shame, manufactured a phony family tree linking us to the British aristocracy."

"There's something else," Bernard said. "You may not be aware, but there's a group known for hunting Nazi war criminals that has asked several countries to compare their bank files with names on its 'most wanted' list—including von Haase.

"The Rosenberg Center in San Francisco is expanding its search to discover the fate of billions of dollars in gold and property confiscated from Holocaust victims. Our bank has already been asked to supply names.

"The center has requested bank searches in Europe and South America. Their idea is to follow the criminals. That's where they'll find the money. It's only a matter of time before the search in Paraguay intensifies and answers come to light. Rumor has it that von Haase fled to Paraguay toward the end of the war."

The priest linked his fingers together. "Sadly, such rumors from my country usually turn out to be facts. I wouldn't be at all surprised if that monster is hidden there…somewhere."

"We'd like to do what no one else has been able to accomplish. Track him down and bring him to trial for his crimes. When that happens, we plan to dissolve the bank, liquidate its assets and give the money to Holocaust survivors and their descendants.

"Naturally, we'd prefer to be the ones to expose our own grandfather before the Rosenberg Center can connect von Haase's money flow with the beginnings of the Taylor World Banking Corporation."

"Ah…" The priest's head went back. "I understand." There was a long moment of quiet. "Does Rickie know she's a von Haase?" he finally asked.

"Yes. She was the one who hired Jordan to hunt him down. But after falling in love with him, she changed her mind."

"I'm presuming she doesn't know you've approached me."

"No. In fact, she'd be very upset if she had any idea. She prefers to leave the situation alone. We gave her our promise we wouldn't ask Stoney or Jordan for help."

"Why come to me?" Father DeSilva asked in a level voice.

Bernard sent Ted a private message through the rearview mirror. Ted nodded.

"Because you were Jordan's contact," he said. "We know you run an underground in the Chaco. You have connections. A map. Rickie told us there's a hideout you had marked called Stroessnerplatz. Apparently you said it's reputed to be a Nazi stronghold, that you're forbidden to do missionary work there.

"She said that when she and Jordan tried to visit, they were turned away at peril of their lives."

The priest gave a troubled sigh. "That's all true."

"We want to get in there and take a look around, Father. Will you help us?"

His dark brows lifted. "Have either of you ever served in the military or trained for combat, like Stoney and Jordan?"

"No," they said in unison.

"Suppose I were to help you, and you got in there only to find that von Haase was not a resident?"

Ted's mouth tightened. "Then we'd ask you to put us in touch with other contacts throughout Paraguay who would know of secret hideouts where he might be found."

"That's what I was afraid you were going to say. You two are on a mission."

"That's right."

"Sometimes a man can get too consumed by a righteous cause, no matter how worthy or noble."

"Tell that to the thousands of innocent Jews he slaughtered in cold blood," Ted reminded him.

Compassion filled the priest's dark eyes. "Your sister was right, you know. It would be better to leave it alone. But—" he raised his hand as Ted was about to object "—it is obvious that the two of you have not been able to rid yourselves of the burden. How tragic for you.

"Let me ask you a question. Take your time before you speak. If you were to put your lives at risk and bring him to justice, if you could give back the money, do you think it would remove the terrible guilt you've taken on?"

They'd pulled to a stop in front of the hotel. This time Bernard was able to turn around. "We can't answer that, Father."

"I can, my sons. The answer lies inside *you*, not your deeds."

His words were reminiscent of Rickie's. Ted bristled. "So you refuse to help us?"

"I didn't say that," the priest murmured. "Bernard, I haven't seen much of the countryside. Why don't you take us for a drive along the river?"

DEBORAH THREW her arms around her brother's waist. "Do you know why I like this apartment?"

"You mean there's something to like? All two square feet of it?"

"Yes, but it's *ours*. And one day we'll be able to afford a bigger place."

"That day better come soon. There's no room for a baby."

"I know. This is just temporary. At least it's near the family and the university."

"Which reminds me, I have to leave in a few minutes. I've got an appointment over there with Marvin. He's arranging a job interview for me with Goldman Documentaries."

"Hey, big brother! You're really coming up in the world if you can work for a director of his caliber."

"It's not a foregone conclusion, but apparently the research I did in Australia for my thesis on Leni Riefenstahl impressed him."

"I remember that name. She was a Nazi filmmaker, right?"

"That's right. A propaganda expert for Hitler. My knowledge of film and photography during that period could be the deciding factor in hiring me."

"You'll get the job. Take my word for it." She

kissed his cheek. "The folks are very proud of you. So am I."

"Thanks, Deborah." He kissed her in return. She felt his gaze lower to the mound visible beneath her cotton shift. "Are you going to be okay here alone for a couple of hours?"

"Of course. We have a bed, a couch, food and a telephone. What more could a pregnant woman want?"

"A lot of things. Like air-conditioning, dressers, tables, lamps, a TV. Space."

"I realize this isn't what you were used to in Canberra, but we'll manage for a while."

"Unfortunately my grant money ran out...." He sighed. "Maybe you should move back home."

"No, David. I told you on the plane. Finding out I'm expecting a baby has made me grow up in a hurry. This apartment represents a new beginning for me. As soon as I can get a job in town, I'll resign from the army and look for a better place to live. Until then, we'll get along."

"If I get this job, we'll have enough money to move next month."

"That would be wonderful. In the meantime, we'll make do. I'm fixing shish kebab for dinner, so don't be late."

"Are you kidding?" The thought of food always brought a smile to her brother's face.

"See you later."

He waved and was soon out the door.

In bare feet she wandered over to the window,

which overlooked the busy street below. Their apartment was three stories up. Not too difficult a climb, but the heat was close to unbearable.

She turned around and rested her back against the sill, surveying her new world. Time to start dinner.

Thank God for David.

She didn't know how she could live in this colorless closet of an apartment without him. When she thought—

No! No more thinking about what might have been.

Weeks ago, before the wedding, she'd given her engagement ring to Rickie, who'd promised to return it to Ted. Removing the diamond from her finger had given her the impetus to throw out every photo, every token, everything he'd ever given her.

The slate had been wiped clean. There were no reminders of him anywhere, nothing but the unwanted images that continually filled her mind—and of course, her own swollen reflection in the mirror.

She couldn't do anything about the baby. She didn't want to. She already adored her son and was determined to be the best mother possible.

However, she could learn to control those mental pictures.

The army had taught her techniques to reduce, even supplant negative images and thought patterns. Why not use them to eradicate memories too bittersweet to bear? she reasoned as the telephone rang.

They'd been hooked up a mere four days. Only her parents and a few close friends knew the number. She hurried over to the kitchen wall to get it. "Hello?"

"Good. You're there."

Deborah took a fortifying breath. Her mother hadn't wanted her to get a place of her own. She claimed it was because she didn't want Deborah spending all her salary on rent; Deborah knew very well that her parents were being protective.

"Where else would I be?" she teased.

"I have something to tell you."

Her mother's nonsensical mood put Deborah on alert. "Go ahead."

"If you're not sitting down, then maybe you should."

Tiny tentacles of fear spread throughout her body. "Is Dad hurt?"

"This has nothing to do with your father."

"Why don't I believe you?"

"You want me to put him on? He's right here."

Deborah smoothed a stray tendril of hair from her cheek. "I'm sitting down, Mom," she lied. There were no chairs.

"Ted was here today. He's on his way over to see you. Right now."

Dear God.

Ted was in Jerusalem?

He was coming to the apartment?

The phone slipped out of her hand. She had to make a lunge so the receiver wouldn't bang against the wall.

"Deborah?" Her mother's frantic voice could be heard through the phone.

Her hand shook as she held the receiver to her ear once more. "I haven't fainted, Mom." Not yet.

"Whatever you do, hear him out."

She blinked.

After everything that had happened, her parents still had the capacity to be civil, even kind to their enemies?

"Why should I?" Her voice shook.

"Just mind your mother, and all will be revealed in good time."

How often, while growing up, had Deborah heard that piece of parental advice and acted on it?

This situation is different from any other.

I can't see him again.

I won't.

You have to.

You told him you were carrying his child.

Now you must hear his response.

"Deborah?"

"I'm going to hang up, Mom."

"You do that. He should be there soon. Don't answer the door without your shoes on."

She closed her eyes tightly before replacing the receiver, then buried her face in her hands.

Even in a crisis—especially in a crisis—her mother never forgot her stupid, stupid little rules that drove the family crazy. Her father said it was her mother's way of coping during times of stress, by doing things like washing the curtains every day or ironing everyone's underwear.

Deborah wished she could lie to herself that her mother had only phoned to ensure that her daughter made herself presentable for company. But Deborah knew that wasn't true.

When Ted had called off their engagement, her mother had also grieved as only a mother can grieve—a mother who deeply loves her daughter, who can feel her joy and her pain.

When Deborah heard footsteps in the stairwell outside, she lifted her head.

Sorry, Mother.
This is one time I can't rise to the occasion.
Ted couldn't give a damn how I look.
I don't give a damn, either.

FROM HIS VANTAGE point on the cement landing, Ted looked out over the section of low-rental housing with distaste. As far as he could tell, there was nothing remarkable about the architecture, nothing about the arrangement of white buildings to recommend it.

He was still trying to recover from his shock that Deborah had already moved into this less-than-adequate apartment complex. With her brother, no less. A grimace stole over his face.

If you decide to go after her, you're in for some emotional trauma of a different sort.

Though he hadn't seen her yet, Ted already had a sinking feeling that his cousin had spoken prophetic words. Otherwise why this unrest he couldn't describe or explain? Why the chilling impression that she'd distanced herself from him in unpleasant ways he had yet to discover?

Sharing an apartment with her brother meant she'd already moved on with her life. Because her stint in Israel's Defense Force, the IDF, kept her away from home a good deal of the time, the move from her parents' house to a place of her own represented a drastic change in the Deborah he'd known before.

Oddly enough, his alarm hadn't grown until the Solomons had informed him that their daughter didn't live with them anymore. An infinitely gracious couple, Deborah's parents were too well-bred to turn him away or demand explanations.

How long had Rickie known about Deborah's pregnancy? Certainly since before her wedding day, or she wouldn't have said all those things to him outside the bathroom door.

He shook his head as if to clear it.

Why does it matter where Deborah's living for the moment? When she hears what you have to say, it will be a moot point.

There was the distinct possibility that David was in the apartment with her. Ted had never met him, but he knew Deborah felt very close to him.

Bernard said her brother had come to the wedding reception with her. Ted had no recollection of it. That night was a blur in his mind.

He had a vague memory of Deborah materializing

in front of him like a heavenly apparition, draped in some silky blue creation. But the news that he was going to be the father of another von Haase had suddenly turned the experience into a nightmare. Like all apparitions, she'd vanished as quickly as she'd come.

Even now, a week later and stone sober, he felt at times that he was still walking on the edge of a strange dream. Nothing would seem real until he saw her again.

He knocked on the door.

"Come in. It's unlocked."

Deborah could say that when she was living in a strange neighborhood where any criminal could just walk in off the streets? Ted frowned angrily. What was she thinking? Especially in her condition.

Unless David was there with her.

Ted didn't like the idea of that, either. He needed time alone with Deborah. If they could've met at her parents' home, he would have been assured of privacy. But this…this shoebox, he mused irritably as he looked around, wouldn't hold him or Deborah comfortably, let alone a third party. For the discussion he had in mind, they would have to go back to his hotel.

With a hardening of his jaw, he let himself inside the minuscule living room-cum-kitchen and shut the door. In one glance he ascertained that if David was around, he was in the bedroom, out of sight.

Ted's searching gaze swerved to the woman standing shoeless at the sink, cutting onions and peppers. He didn't recognize the café-au-lait-colored sundress that left her golden arms and legs bare. But she had confined her glistening brown hair in the familiar thick braid that hung down her back.

There was nothing he loved more than to undo it as a prelude to making love. Every time the satiny texture slithered over his hands and swirled to her waist, he was reminded that a woman's hair truly was her crowning glory. Especially in Deborah's case, where the same rich color was reflected in her darkly fringed eyes and expressive brows, exquisitely arched and defined.

Those features were combined with a wide mouth, proud nose and the most beautiful olive skin; he could never stop kissing or touching it. She was like his own private sun, radiating life-giving warmth.

No woman had ever projected such powerful magnetism for him. From their first meeting, she'd filled all the empty spaces of his existence, redefined the meaning of his life.

"Sit down, Ted." She spoke without turning around. "Mother said you were on your way over. Just a minute and I'll be finished making dinner. When David gets back from the university, he'll be starving."

So David wasn't here, after all. The news pleased him, but his pleasure was short-lived.

"If you're thirsty," she said chattily, as if he were a next-door neighbor who'd dropped in for a quick visit, "there's beer in the refrigerator. Help yourself."

She'd punished him enough. Impatient to get her in his arms, he closed the distance between them in a few swift strides and lifted his hands to her shoulders. As he started to knead them, delicious warmth seeped into his fingers.

Mingled with the astringent odor of the onions, he caught the sweet scent of the soap she always used.

"Please don't touch me," she began in a low voice. "We're no longer engaged. We're no longer anything."

"I beg to differ," he whispered against the moist skin of her neck, sliding his hands down her back and around the front of her body. He knew every breathtaking line and curve. She had thickened, and was surprisingly hard.

He urged her closer, but she didn't melt against him like she'd always done before. In a startling move, she pivoted away from him.

He had to let her go while she reached in the refrigerator for a package of cubed lamb.

"Too bad your jaded world has made you so distrusting, Ted. You obviously didn't believe I was pregnant." She flashed him a brief, pitying glance before she started putting the meat and vegetables on skewers.

What in the hell was she talking about?

CHAPTER FOUR

DEBORAH PUT the loaded skewers in a pan and placed it under the broiler, then stood up and looked at him without hesitation. "I guess the dress I wore to Rickie's wedding camouflaged me better than I thought. Either that or the alcohol blunted your perception."

"Deborah—"

"I should've remembered that a renowned banker like yourself never talks serious business without first spiking his guns with all the facts at his disposal.

"So now you know for sure I'm pregnant. You've touched me...and the baby. But if you think you can dictate future negotiations, I have news for you. As I told you at the reception, I don't want anything from you.

"The one and only reason I showed up was because I knew it was my legal and moral obligation to inform you of my pregnancy. If and when the day ever arrives that you want to acknowledge your son, instruct one of your attorneys to get in touch with mine, Isaac Solomon. You've met my uncle. He'll be handling all my affairs from now on.

"That was the other piece of information I would

have shared with you after the reception, if you'd shown the slightest degree of interest, which of course you didn't.

"Darling—"

"Now I'm claiming the same privilege."

He was convinced she hadn't heard the endearment. Lord. There was a time in the not-so-distant past when it would have propelled her into his arms. His rejection of her had changed her into someone he didn't know.

"For the record, I do not want to see you or talk to you again. Not in this lifetime or the next. I would appreciate it if you'd leave."

He saw the defiance in her eyes, felt it in her stance. So far, he could find no hint of vulnerability.

"I'm not ready to go yet."

Her brows lifted in the same intimidating gesture he'd seen her father use on occasion. "You want a verbal commitment from me stating that I won't come after you for your money? Is that what this is all about?"

"Don't, Deborah."

On the way over to her apartment, he'd thought that if he gave her the opportunity to vent all the hurt and anger stored inside, she would eventually break down. At that point he would tell her why he'd ended their engagement.

It wouldn't be the truth, of course, but it would provide an explanation he felt she'd accept so that he could propose marriage to her for the second time.

But their conversation had taken a different turn, increasing his anxiety. He could feel her slipping away from him.

"Don't what?" Her mouth curved into an icy smile. He hadn't known she could look like that. "Your money never meant anything to me. You even had me convinced it didn't mean anything to you. No wonder you went to so much trouble to make certain I stayed away from Graycliff."

Baffled, confused by her erroneous assumptions, he muttered, "Graycliff?"

"The Taylor family estate. You never invited me there. Now I know the reason. You didn't have any intention of marrying me, and you didn't want me to see what kind of house you lived in—how much money you had. It might give me ideas."

Ted groaned under the weight of the damage inflicted by his silent rejection.

"In my naiveté, I believed you when you said you were estranged from your mother and father, and that was why you didn't want me meeting them until after our wedding.

"Isn't it interesting that there must have been at least two thousand people at the reception, most of whom you had to know, standing there smiling and shaking hands with your mother and father? From my vantage point it all looked like one big happy family."

Ted took a shuddering breath. "You don't understand."

"Of course not. My job wasn't to understand,

only to warm your bed until you grew bored with me.''

His anger reached its flash point. He gripped her upper arms, bringing her up tight against his body. ''Don't you ever say that again!''

She didn't flinch. ''Well, if that's not the reason you dropped me, then maybe it's because my last name is Solomon. In the beginning you didn't let on that it bothered you.

''How galling it must be to realize that despite every effort to protect yourself, you've accidentally made a child who has the blood of Judah running through his veins.''

''Deborah!'' he cried out in desperation, crushing her to him.

Her body remained rigid.

He'd known his rejection of her would hurt for a long time, but he'd never dreamed her pain would reach these agonizing depths. If he didn't do something quickly, she could be scarred for life. He couldn't live another day with her existing in this kind of hell.

''Let me go, Ted. Don't force me to use a technique I've learned in the army. It might hurt my son.''

Her words filled him with fresh despair. He slowly relinquished his hold of her and stepped back.

''I want you to leave,'' she said stiffly.

He raked an unsteady hand through his hair. ''I'm not going anywhere. We have to talk.''

Her eyes narrowed in disdain. "That's what I used to say to you, over and over again. For days and weeks and months, I left those words on your answering machines. I said them in letters, I wrote them in faxes. There was never a reply." She drew in long draughts of air. "Now I have nothing to say to you. Goodbye, Ted."

He had no intention of leaving.

"My sister has asked you to get out. In the nicest possible way, of course. I suggest you do so."

Ted hadn't heard David come in. One glimpse, and he could see Deborah's mother in the other man's attractive features.

"I'm glad you're here, David. I've always wanted to meet the brother Deborah adores."

David's face screwed up in repulsion. "You arrogant swine. How dare you show up here? Who the bloody hell do you think you are?"

Ted could feel the other man's venom. He didn't blame him. If their situations had been reversed, Ted would have tackled David to the floor by now. His forebearance underlined the Solomons' good breeding.

"For one, I'm the father of your unborn nephew. That gives me the right to be here." He saw a movement of the other man's throat. "For another, I plan to make Deborah my wife as soon as it can be arranged."

He heard Deborah's gasp from the tiny kitchen. It told him he'd finally made some kind of breakthrough, fragile and precarious though it was. Thank God.

"For another, your parents gave me permission to speak to her."

"But Deborah didn't give you her permission," he said, fighting back with touching valor. Deborah had a champion in her sibling. Ted was eminently glad of it.

"I thought she did by her appearance at the wedding reception—or was I wrong?"

Ted's comment quieted her brother for the moment.

"As I was saying to her before you came in, we need to talk things out. Deborah?"

He turned to her, but once again she was busy, taking dinner out of the oven.

"There were reasons I broke off our engagement. But the news of the baby changes everything. I'm now prepared to reveal those reasons.

"When you're ready to hear them, phone me at the Jerusalem Towers. I'm not leaving the city until we've had our talk."

He nodded at her bemused brother on his way out the door.

If she didn't make an appearance at the hotel before morning, Ted had one more ace up his sleeve. Deborah's parents. He disliked using them, but he would if he was forced.

The situation had grown desperate.

"AREN'T YOU GOING to eat your dinner? I went to a lot of trouble to make it."

David wandered into the kitchen area. "I know you did. It looks delicious. Deborah?"

Here it comes.

"Are you going to call him?"

Her hands clung to the edge of the sink. "No."

"Good." He pounded his fist on the countertop. "I'd like to see that bastard stew in his own juice and find out what it feels like."

It's a living death.

"He'd have to have a hell of a good reason for doing what he did to you. I don't think he does. He believes that if he can lure you to the hotel, he can lure you into his bed again. Then all will be forgiven."

She shook her head. "That's not going to happen. Marriage is out of the question. Deep down he knows it. In fact, he's counting on my rejecting him. But he has to go through with this charade the same way I did when I showed up at the reception. We both had a duty to fulfill for our baby's sake.

"Now that we've played the game, he'll grow impatient of the wait and leave Jerusalem for good."

"That day can't come soon enough."

"Never fear. Ted Taylor is involved in the kind of business that runs the banking world. It won't be able to get along twenty-four hours without him. By this time tomorrow night he'll be flying back to New York."

"Deborah?"

She sucked in her breath. "What?"

"Do you think you'll ever get over him?"

Please don't ask me a question like that. She looked into David's eyes.

"I'm sorry." He reached for his food and went over to the couch to eat.

"It's okay. Ask me again in fifty years and maybe I'll be able to answer."

"BENJAMIN? MIRIAM?" Ted shook the hands of both Solomons. "I appreciate your seeing me on such short notice this morning. But it's vitally urgent that I speak with you."

"Come in the study and sit down."

With a sensation like déjà vu, Ted followed them down the hallway to his favorite room in their home. It housed hundreds of books of all kinds, and he'd always found it fascinating to peruse the shelves.

Benjamin, retired after a career in the IDF, was currently engaged in writing a series of technical manuals for the army. Certain days of the week, he and Miriam worked at the Holocaust memorial. The rest of the time they spent with their extended family.

Ted suspected they were a little lonely with both children gone from the house. But they always found meaningful ways to fill their time and serve others. Their outgoing friendliness was one of the traits that drew Ted to them and made him feel more than a guest.

"Would you care for tea or coffee?"

"Nothing, thank you."

Deborah's father, a large man with silvering hair,

indicated the love seat before he sank down in his easy chair. Miriam, his lovely wife, perched on the edge of a straight-backed chair placed near the coffee table, her hands clasped in her lap.

Ted realized this impromptu visit had made both of them anxious, but it wasn't in their nature to pry. He hoped that before he was through telling them his carefully constructed apology, their minds would be set at ease.

"You found the children's apartment without any trouble?"

"I did. Thank you very much. When I arrived, Deborah was making shish kebabs."

"My Deborah is a wonderful cook."

Ted smiled at her. "She takes after her mother." It was the truth. He'd eaten some of the best food in his life at the Solomon table.

"Before I left the apartment, I had the pleasure of meeting David. He looks like you, Miriam." Her brown eyes lit up. "I already like him because he takes good care of your daughter."

Benjamin nodded. "They've always been close, like you and your sister."

Like my sister and I used to be.

"I'm here because I love your daughter and want to marry her. It's true that hearing about the baby caused me to reenter her life. If she hadn't come to Rickie's wedding reception to tell me she was pregnant, I wouldn't be here now. But the baby is a fact of life, and I want to be the one to raise him with Deborah."

Her parents sat motionless.

"You both know my background. There was no religion in our home. I am not a religious person. I don't believe in a higher power. Organized religions seem pointless to me.

"When I fell in love with Deborah, religion didn't come into the picture. I loved her for herself and looked forward to married life with her. She said she was willing to enter into a mixed marriage. I took her at her word and never gave it another thought.

"The last time she was in New York with me, we met with a Rabbi Arnavitz. You may recall that he was going to perform the wedding ceremony."

They nodded solemnly.

"What Deborah doesn't know is that after she left to fly back to Jerusalem, the rabbi called me into his office for further talks. At first I thought he was trying to convert me and I must admit it bothered me. But out of respect for Deborah, I sat there and listened.

"To my surprise, he asked me a question. Did I understand the kind of sacrifice Deborah was making to become my wife? I didn't know what he meant and told him so. That's when my education in Judaism began."

Up to this point, everything he'd told them was the truth. Now for the lie...

"What he did was paint such a moving picture for me, I eventually came to the conclusion that no matter how much I loved her or she loved me, something would be missing in her marriage if I didn't convert. That meant accepting the Obligation of the Commandments.''

Benjamin nodded. Both of them had tears in their eyes.

"After a great deal of soul-searching, I have to confess that I couldn't in all honesty make that commitment. I also came to the conclusion that the best way to honor Deborah was to let her go. I knew if I did, in time she'd find a good man of her own faith and culture—a husband who'd worship with her.

"Because I knew how much we loved each other, I could conceive of only one way to end the relationship, and that was to be cruel to her. Anything short of that would not have created the necessary break.'' He could feel his whole body shaking. "My plan would have worked if—"

"If God had not had another purpose in mind!" Miriam finished for him. She got up from the chair and rushed over to him, resting her hands on both his cheeks. "I knew there had to a good reason! I knew it. Didn't I tell you?" She looked at her husband.

"Are you saying you are now ready to convert?" Benjamin inquired in an emotional voice.

They took their measure of each other.

"No. But I'm more in love with your daughter than ever, and I'm prepared to have our son raised Jewish. I'll do everything in my power to support him and Deborah in their religious life. I intend to be the best husband and father I can be...if Deborah will have me. Last night she told me goodbye. She meant it.''

Silence filled the room.

''I told her she could reach me at the Jerusalem Towers if she wanted to talk. When she made no effort to phone or visit me, I came to the conclusion that she had no intention of doing so.

''I've decided to return to New York. If she never contacts me again, I'll stay in touch with the family through your brother, Isaac. Rest assured that Deborah and our son will always be provided for. In fact, the second I get back, I'll instruct my attorney to make funds available to her.

''She'll probably refuse the money, but if she does that, then I'll be denied any part in my son's life. That thought is unacceptable to me. Also, she'll be denying me the possibility of making restitution for the pain I've caused her and your family. So, I'm depending on you to make sure the money is used to provide for Deborah and the baby.

''Because of my behavior, I have no one to blame but myself for everything that's happened.'' He rose to his feet, unable to sit there any longer. It pained him to lie to them, but he had no other choice.

''Thank you for listening. You've been the parents I longed for. Because I honor you, I felt you had the right to know what really happened and why. I love you both,'' he added. It was only the truth. ''Please don't get up. I'll see myself out.''

This time it was a wrench leaving their home. If

Deborah didn't change her mind, he would never have the right to come here again. Another loss.

He hurried outside to the waiting taxi and instructed the driver to take him to the airport. En route he made a call to Bernard on his cellular phone.

"What's the verdict?" his cousin asked.

Ted had a suffocating feeling in his chest. "I don't know yet. For now, it's a waiting game."

"As long as you don't know, there's still hope."

The scene in Deborah's kitchen had been a waking nightmare. By contrast, he felt good about his visit with the Solomons. Only time would tell how good he had any right to feel. At the moment, Ted wasn't optimistic. The damage might have gone too deep. He felt ill.

"I'll be back in New York this evening."

"Good. Come by my condo on your way in. There's been a development. Father DeSilva phoned last night. We have to let him know the exact date we can be in Asunción to meet one of his contacts."

So the priest was going to come through for them, after all. A surge of adrenaline kicked in.

"I needed that news."

"I thought you might. Hurry home."

"COME ON, DEBORAH. We're going to be late for Shabbat. Dad's waiting at the door."

She and David raced up the steps to their parents' home. They'd cut it close this time.

"Hurry into the dining room. Your mother is ready to light the Sabbath candles."

"Sorry, Mom," Deborah whispered as she placed the lace covering over her head. "My last job interview took longer than I expected."

"I haven't seen you all week and then you come late. We'll talk about it after."

The four of them assembled around the table where Deborah's mother had placed the glass candlesticks. Upon lighting them, they covered their eyes.

"Baruch Ata, Ado-nai Elo-heinu Melech Ha'olam, asher kid'shanu b'mitzvotav v'tzivanu l'hadlik ner shel Shabbat." Blessed are You, Lord our God, King of the Universe, Who has sanctified us with His commandments and commanded us to light the Shabbat lights.

Deborah uncovered her eyes too soon. Her mother had begun a personal family prayer. They were usually long. She saw the twinkle in David's eye before she lowered her head once more.

"We are thankful to be gathered together as one. We are thankful for the safe arrival of our David from Australia. May he be blessed in his pursuits.

"We are thankful for our Deborah who will be the mother of a fine son before the end of the year. May she and the baby stay healthy and strong.

"We ask You to remember the baby's father, Ted, who wishes to become Deborah's husband and has made his commitment before us and You to raise their son according to Your law.

"May Deborah be guided to grant him his wish and obey Your will.

"May all Israel receive of your blessings, Lord our God."

Deborah gasped, stunned by the words of her mother's prayer. She slowly pulled the covering from her head and folded it in the buffet drawer.

"This is nice," their father said as she rejoined them at the dinner table. His dark eyes shone with pride as he surveyed them one by one in the soft glow of candlelight. "David? It's good to have you back. This home has been empty without our children, eh, Miriam?"

There was a deafening silence.

Try as she might, Deborah couldn't hold back the tears. "When did Ted tell you all those things, Mom?"

"On Monday morning, before he left to fly back to New York."

Five days ago. He didn't even last the full twenty-four hours.

She used her napkin to wipe the moisture from her cheeks. "He never said them to me."

"Did you give him the chance?" her father inquired mildly.

"He doesn't love me."

Her mother faced her squarely. "He loved you so much, he didn't want your marriage to a non-Jew to take away from your greatest happiness under the law. After a long discussion with Rabbi Arnavitz, he sacrificed his own desires for your sake. He didn't have to do that. His was the greater love. He tried to make you forget him in the only way he knew how."

"Your mother speaks the truth, Deborah. But having learned about the baby, he is ready to assume his rightful place as your husband and your baby's father. He doesn't have intentions at this time of converting. Not yet..." Her father added his own interpretation. "But he will allow our grandson to be raised as you were raised. Under the law."

She took a shuddering breath. "This is what you want me to do?"

Her father's hands went up in the air in characteristic fashion. The gesture could mean anything from elation to frustration. "No man or woman can decide for another. The truth is, we like him."

"We do, Deborah," her mother chimed in.

"We always have."

"We always will."

"Excuse me." Deborah practically knocked over her chair, getting up from the table. David wasn't far behind as he followed her into her old bedroom.

She dove onto the bed, burying her face in the cushions. But she paid an immediate price because she'd forgotten she was pregnant. The pain forced her to sit up.

David sat down beside her and held her for a moment.

How could she have forgotten her condition when it was the existence of the baby that had precipitated this latest crisis?

"Are you all right?"

"I don't think I'm ever going to be all right again."

"Mom and Dad would never force you to marry him. You know that."

She turned her head toward him. "Do you believe what he said to them? All that stuff about not wanting to come between me and Judaism?"

He pondered the question. "I don't know. From what Rickie told me, the two of them were raised without any kind of religion or belief system. Maybe Ted felt he couldn't live up to you. I suppose he could have had an attack of conscience because he knew he'd never convert and feared it would hurt you."

"Just answer me with a simple yes or no."

"Honestly?"

She nodded.

"Then, no. I just don't think most people are that noble."

"I don't, either."

"Whatever his real agenda, he obviously changed his mind and came back for you and the baby."

"For all of twelve hours. So where does that leave me?"

"From the parents' point of view, alone, unwed, pregnant. Unhappy."

"Thanks a lot, brother dear."

"You wanted the truth."

Her eyes filled again. "I count on you for the truth."

"You haven't asked me what I think you should do yet."

Deborah got up from the bed and started to pace. She didn't respond.

"Then I'll tell you. I think that not very many people experience a great love in their lives. Little loves, maybe, but not the big soul-destroying, flames burning, wretched kind that brands you forever and always."

"You think that's the kind of love Ted and I have." That was exactly how it felt.

"I know it is," he said with unswerving conviction. It sent chills down her spine.

"I don't like him, Deborah. But I can't deny what I saw and felt around the two of you in the apartment. If I was lucky enough to be given a second chance at that kind of love, I'd probably close my eyes and leap."

"Deborah?"

Her parents stood in the doorway of her room. "We came to tell you we love you."

"I know. I love you, too."

David was trying to hold back a smile. He knew why their parents were just standing there, waiting....

"All right!" Deborah cried out in exasperation. "The answer to your question is yes. There's going to be a wedding."

Her parents broke into laughter, then tears. Before long her father had put his arms around her mother.

He danced her across the room like a man half his age.

The words are out. You've said them to your parents. That's like saying them to God. The only person left to tell is Ted.

What have I done?

CHAPTER FIVE

AT FOUR O'CLOCK on Sunday afternoons, the Church of Santa Lucia in Asunción offered confession in Spanish, Guaraní, English, German and French.

The large religious edifice in the center of the capital city boasted a magnificent shrine to the Holy Virgin, reputed to have been a gift from a doge of the former republic of Venice to the bishop of Paraguay.

The church catered to a huge body of locals as well as the thousands of visitors who flocked there from all parts of South America and the rest of the world.

While Bernard blended in with other sightseers to view the stained-glass windows, Ted stood in the English-speaking line behind a crowd of tourists from New Zealand. His impatience to make this first contact was superseded only by his need to know if he had overestimated the strength of the Solomons' affection for him.

No word from Deborah in seven days could mean one of two things. Either her parents had decided to say nothing to their daughter because ultimately it would be best for her to find a Jewish husband.

Or the second possibility, the one he feared most,

was that the Solomons' influence on her didn't extend far enough to convince Deborah to forgive him.

When he'd learned of his relationship to von Haase, he'd had no choice but to shut her out. Given the same situation again, he would do exactly the same thing without compunction. But the existence of the baby couldn't be ignored. Oddly enough, he'd thought that her condition would have made her more vulnerable to accepting his second marriage proposal.

How wrong could he have been? The change in her was so dramatic, he still hadn't recovered.

The warm, loving woman he remembered, the generous, passionate woman he'd known only months ago, was nowhere in evidence. Standing at that kitchen sink with her back toward him, she'd been immune to any attempts he'd made, physically or otherwise, to find a crack in her veneer.

Bernard wasn't the kind of person to say "I told you so," but Ted wouldn't have blamed him for thinking it. The truth of the matter was, Deborah might never respond to him except through her attorney. That possibility was tearing him apart.

He felt a nudge against his arm—the tourist who'd just vacated the confessional alerting him that it was his turn. With this visit to Paraguay so vital to his and Bernard's plan, he felt angry that his preoccupation with Deborah had resulted in someone having to remind him where he was.

Thanking the elderly woman, he entered the cubicle and knelt down. Father DeSilva had told him the exact wording to use. "Bless me Father for I have sinned," he said through the little grate.

"How long has it been since your last confession?" Whoever was speaking English had a strong Spanish accent.

"I spoke with Father DeSilva very recently. He sent me to talk to you, Father."

There was a long pause. "Did you come alone?"

"No. My cousin is with me."

"What is his name?"

"Bernard?"

"Do you have any idea how many Nazi hunters have swarmed into Paraguay over the years looking for your grandfather?"

"I can imagine. Have they searched for him in Stroessnerplatz?"

"They've tried, but have never been successful. That area has been off-limits to the public for close to fifty years."

If von Haase had been close to forty years of age when he'd disappeared, that put him in his late eighties today. The time frame fit.

"Why the inaccessibility, Father?"

"Over the years it has been the reputed stronghold of ousted dictators from other countries. Not only Nazis but power-crazed military leaders operating outside the law. Most recently, it is believed to the be the headquarters of General Oriana."

"Didn't he lead an unsuccessful coup against the current dictator three years ago?"

"That's right. Rumor has it that he is planning

another one sometime in the future. The compound is fortified against intruders.''

Rickie and Jordan had found that out when they'd pretended to be honeymooners exploring the Chaco and had come face-to-face with one of the guards.

"Who funds him?" No one knew better than Ted that it took a lot of untraceable money to finance a military junta like Oriana's.

It was more than possible that von Haase's blood money was responsible for underwriting many subversive activities among the criminal element in Paraguay. Ted could imagine the scenario. "General? You're welcome here. I'll be happy to supply you with arms and ammunition. Anything you need. In return, you will continue to protect me from the world.''

"There are businessmen in our country who don't like the current dictator's policies and want him removed at any price.''

"How would I go about getting word to Oriana that I'm one of those men with certain vested interests who might like to talk over a private business venture with him?''

"That would be very dangerous.''

"It will provide me with the only entrée I can conceive of to get inside the compound and take a good look around. Do you know someone?'' Ted persisted.

"There is a Dr. Arbizu at Government Hospital who has been known to treat Oriana from time to time for an old wound he received during a military campaign.''

''You think he's a sympathizer?''

''If he weren't, he would be dead.''

That was all Ted needed to hear. ''Thank you, Father. I will find a way to repay you through Father DeSilva.''

''You may not live long enough to do that.''

''You underestimate my incentive.''

The possibility of bringing von Haase in alive is the only thing that sustains me. It's the only reason I can contemplate marriage to the woman I've defiled.

''Then God be with you, my son.''

''And you, Father.''

Ted rose from his kneeling position and left the confessional, eager to discuss everything with Bernard, who'd already gone outside and hailed them a taxi. No sooner had he climbed in the back and shut the door than his cousin's brows lifted in silent query. Ted's gaze darted him a private message indicating the meeting had been successful.

''Hotel Guaraní, *por favor, señor.*''

''*Sí, señor.*''

As they sped toward their destination, Ted quietly related the details of his conversation with the priest. By the time they'd gotten out of the atrocious heat and back to the blessed relief of their air-conditioned hotel, they'd devised a plan to meet with Dr. Arbizu. But Ted couldn't get Deborah off his mind.

''I'm going to call New York to see if there are

any messages for us." He picked up the receiver of their hotel phone. His cellular didn't work from Paraguay to the States.

Bernard crossed their hotel room and reached into the minibar for a couple of cold bottles of mineral water. He handed one to Ted. "Any luck?"

"I'm not sure. There's a call from Jerusalem, but I don't recognize the number." Hearing the 972 country code for Israel had sent the adrenaline rushing through his body. The additional 2 indicated Jerusalem, but it wasn't her parents' number. He'd memorized that a long time ago.

Perspiration beaded his forehead. Was it the phone in Deborah's apartment, or had she instructed her uncle to call, wanting to know the name of Ted's attorney so they could set up financial and visitation terms?

"Before you die of curiosity, why not call the number back?" Bernard could always read Ted's mind. "Our other business can wait until I've finished my shower."

Ted muttered his thanks. It was six in the evening here, which meant it was midnight in Jerusalem.

The phone call must have been placed within the last two hours. After coming in from the airport that morning, he and Bernard had stayed in their hotel room all day, discussing strategies. She hadn't phoned his office before they left for the church, because he'd checked.

His heart resumed its hammering. Something told him it was Deborah, not her Uncle Isaac. For one thing, Ted realized that Isaac wouldn't conduct business at night, let alone on the Sabbath. *It had to be Deborah.*

It had been a week since they'd spoken in her apartment. Using his calling card, he punched in the numbers and waited.

"THE PHONE'S ringing!"

"Will you answer it, David? I'm brushing my teeth."

Deborah was tired and couldn't handle another conversation with her mother. She'd phoned the apartment three times in the last couple of hours wanting to know if Ted had returned Deborah's call to New York.

How many times had Deborah told her mother that Ted could be anywhere, doing anything? It might be several days or more before she heard back from him.

She'd called his cellular phone, his condo and the office. All she'd gotten was voice mail. She hadn't left messages, knowing that he would have access to her number; records were kept of all numbers that called his office link. Besides, what she had to say wasn't easily stated in a brief, impersonal message.

Since she'd fallen in love with him, Deborah's emotions had gone through so many transitions, she didn't honestly know how she felt about him anymore.

They could never go back to the way things once were.

He'd admitted to her parents that he wouldn't have gotten in touch with her again if it hadn't been for the baby. She couldn't imagine what kind of marriage they could achieve under these circumstances.

Her parents might not have forced her to accept Ted's proposal, but the alternative of her remaining unmarried, having her baby alone, gave them a lot of anxiety, especially as they were growing older and wanted to see her settled.

Of course they were proud people. But not to a fault. They wouldn't want her to marry him just to save face. Her parents were practical, not superficial. They were looking at the situation squarely.

To their way of thinking, Deborah had loved Ted enough to have a baby with him. Whatever had caused him to break off with her, he was back, ready to assume the duties of husband and father. That had to account for a great deal. Enough to make a marriage work, they reasoned.

But no one except Deborah and Ted would actually have to live in that marriage. No one would know what life was going to be like behind closed doors. No one would know how hard it was going to be to bind herself legally to this man when he hadn't wanted her the first time around.

Taking him back when he'd never really been hers was an act of blind faith, and all for the sake of their unborn baby.

He had promised to support her in raising their

son in her faith. She didn't think he would make that promise without planning to keep it.

On the other hand, she hadn't thought he could write her a letter that would practically destroy her, either. At this point she had no idea who Ted really was. She only knew that he'd brought her the greatest joy and the greatest pain of her existence.

How much more pain lay ahead?

That was an absurd question when she already knew the answer. A lifetime's worth—because she wasn't the woman he'd wanted to end up marrying.

"Deborah?" Her brother knocked before poking his head inside the bathroom. "It's Ted."

Oddly enough, now that she'd made the decision to marry him, her heart didn't pound out of control at the mention of his name, the way it used to. If anything, she felt dull on the inside, resigned.

She put her toothbrush away, wiped her mouth on the towel and padded into the kitchen. David gave her shoulder a squeeze before he disappeared into the bedroom.

"Hello, Ted."

"Darling?"

That doesn't mean anything to me anymore, Ted, but if you want to pretend it does, then I'll let you cling to your delusions.

"Yes?"

"Thank God," he murmured. "I'm sorry I wasn't where I could be reached when you called. A business meeting kept Bernard and me tied up until now."

Already he was telling a lie. Ted always kept his cellular phone with him. No matter where he was— Los Angeles or Switzerland or…or wherever—he would have known who was calling and when. That meant he'd needed the two hours since she'd phoned to decide if he really wanted to go through with this marriage charade or not.

Were you with another woman, Ted? Were you hoping I wouldn't take you up on your marriage proposal?

Until their breakup, he'd given her no reason to believe he could be interested in anyone else. But after what had happened, she realized he was capable of anything.

If he'd been seeing someone else when he wasn't in Jerusalem with her, and it had turned into a full-blown love affair, then Deborah could understand how news of the baby had complicated his life. And the other woman's…if there was one.

"Deborah?" There was an unmistakable ring of intimacy in his tone now. "You'll never know what it meant to me to get back here and realize you'd phoned."

His voice had lowered, the way it did when he was caught up in passion. It was hard to believe there'd been a time when she'd responded to that passion with her entire being.

"You *are* going to marry me!"

What a wonderful actor you are, Ted. You sound like you did the first time you proposed to me.

"I thought you'd realize that when you saw that I'd called."

"Except that I didn't recognize the number."

"Who else would be trying to reach you from Jerusalem?"

"Don't tease me, darling." He actually seemed upset. "I can't handle that right now. To be truthful, I can't wait to see you again, to hold you. It's been so long, Deborah."

She took a deep breath and leaned against the wall to ease the ache in her back. "When do you want to get married?"

"As soon as possible. In Jerusalem. I want to start our marriage out right."

"That isn't possible, Ted. Only Orthodox rabbis are certified to perform marriages here. Ours will be an intermarriage. That's why I suggested we be married in New York in the first place."

"I thought that agreeing to raise our son in your faith would change things."

"No. At least if we get married in the States your friends and family can be there, especially your parents."

"Forget my parents. I don't want them there because they have nothing to do with us. Do you understand?"

"Yes."

"Please believe me when I say I want to honor you, Deborah."

Dear God, how I wish that was true.

"You'll be honoring me by giving our son your name. It doesn't matter where we're married."

"Can we still have a Jewish wedding, with all your family there?"

"Of course. We'll arrange it with Rabbi Arnavitz."

"We can break the glass?"

Deborah felt a pain deep in her heart. She'd taken him to a friend's wedding in Jerusalem. He'd seemed to love every minute of it.

At this point, she didn't know when he was acting and when he was real. This would be her torment every day from now on. "We can discuss the details later," she said brusquely.

"When?" he demanded. "If you've already found a job, you'll have to quit. I want you in New York with me as soon as possible."

It was time to end the conversation.

"I could probably fly over on Wednesday."

That should give you a little more room to breathe and straighten out your private affairs....

"That's four days from now. I don't know if I can last that long," he said in a husky voice. He sighed. "All right. Wednesday. I'll book you on the earliest flight. Your tickets will be waiting for you at the El Al counter."

"All right. If that's everything—"

"Deborah? Don't hang up yet."

"I'm afraid I have to," she lied. "David needs to use the phone."

"For how long?"

"I don't know."

"I'll call you back."

"That isn't necessary. We'll be seeing each other next week."

There was a tense silence.

"Expect to hear from me in a little while. We haven't even begun to talk about the things that need to be said."

The line went dead.

Deborah hung up the receiver.

It's too late for talk, Ted. I'm afraid everything was said in that letter you sent me. The words are engraved in my memory.

Dear Deborah,

It seems strange to be writing you a letter when we've only ever used the phone to communicate during our times apart.

There is no easy way to say this, so I'll just say it.

I'm calling off our engagement because I've come to the realization that I'm not in love with you.

Don't ever blame yourself. This has nothing to do with you and everything to do with me.

I don't want the ring back.

May your god bless you and your family always.

Ted.

"Deborah?" Her brother wandered into the kitchen. "Has that bastard said or done anything else to upset you?''

"No." She shook her head. "It's nothing like that. We talked, and I told him I'd marry him. He's expecting me to fly to New York on Wednesday.''

"If everything's all right, then how come you look so...so pale?''

"Probably because I'm pregnant.''

"Deborah— Tell me what's wrong.''

"Nothing's wrong. That's the trouble. If you could've heard Ted just now, you would have thought he was the man I first fell in love with, the man I thought was in love with me.''

David took off his glasses to rub the bridge of his nose. "I told you Friday night that the two of you share something very special—despite everything that's happened.''

Her hands formed into fists. "I don't want to get swallowed alive again, David. Especially if there's another woman.''

"Did he tell you there was?''

"No. But how else do you explain our breakup?''

"You have no proof he was ever unfaithful.''

"I realize that," she said in a trembling voice. "David, I told him I had to get off the phone so you could use it. He'll be calling me again in a few minutes. I don't want to talk to him.''

"But you're going to be spending the rest of your life with him!''

"I know.''

She felt her brother's arms go around her. "I

don't blame you for being terrified of getting hurt again,'' he whispered, ''but try not to imagine things that might not be true. Remember, you're doing this for your child.''

So is he. He's simply doing a better job of pretending than I am.

''Shall I tell him when he calls that you've—''

The phone rang before the rest of the sentence was out. This time her heart was pounding fast, too fast.

''I'll get it.'' She reached decisively for the receiver and said hello.

''Deborah? I've decided I don't want to wait until Wednesday to see you. I've made reservations to fly in on Tuesday. I'll come straight to your apartment from the airport.''

She panicked. ''I'll be busy on Tuesday, getting my packing done.''

''That's why I'm coming. At this stage in your pregnancy you need help, and you shouldn't be traveling on your own.''

''I've gotten along fine so far.''

''I want to take care of you. Don't deny me that privilege.''

Her eyes closed tightly.

''Have you decided to name our son David, after your brother?'' he teased, obviously eager to change the subject.

How can you be this natural with me when a week ago you were never going to see me again?

''No. Since his middle name will be Solomon, I

thought you should be the one to pick out his first name. Maybe he should be called Theodore, after you. We could shorten it to Ted, Jr. Or Teddy.

"If you don't like that, maybe you should pick a good solid English name from your own family. John or Joseph, maybe.

"What about George, after your grandfather?" She could hear herself talking faster and faster and couldn't seem to stop. She realized she was on the verge of hysteria.

"George Solomon Taylor would be a name to be proud of," she rattled on. "Of course I really like Alexander, after your father. We could call him Alex."

He was silent so long, she thought he hadn't heard her.

"Ted?"

As the silence wore on, she remembered too late that he never liked to talk about his father. How could she have forgotten?

"I'm sorry I said something to upset you."

"Don't ever apologize, Deborah," he said quietly. "It's not your fault." Did just the mention of his father create the kind of pain she'd heard just now? "I'm afraid I'm the one who got us on the subject in the first place. If you want to know the truth, I'd rather you chose one of your own family names."

He was perfectly serious. Obviously the thought of this baby brought him no joy. It made her wonder if he would remain aloof from their son after he was born.

If Ted's father couldn't show him love, then it was possible he wouldn't be able to show love to their son. Psychological studies had strong data to prove such a theory. The thought made her go cold inside.

"Ted, there's plenty of time to decide on a name. We'll worry about it later."

"You sound tired, darling. Go to bed. We'll talk again before I see you on Tuesday. Good night. Sleep well."

"Good night."

"Is THERE GOING to be a wedding?"

Ted lifted his head from his hands, staring at Bernard through bleary eyes. His cousin had showered and dressed while he was on the phone with Deborah.

"Yes."

"Then why the despair?"

"I made the mistake of asking her if she'd thought up a name for our son. She said I should be the one to choose it. Something from the English side of our family. A good, fine name to make us both proud," he spat out. "Like George. Or Alexander."

Bernard pursed his lips. "Today we're a step closer to erasing our shame. The first item of business is to make contact with the good doctor."

"You do it while I shower, will you?"

Within five minutes Ted had washed off the sweat and grime. What a pity one couldn't get rid of shame in the same fast, effortless manner.

Curious to know what Bernard had found out, he left the bathroom with a towel hitched around his hips. "What did you find out?"

"Dr. Arbizu spends one week of every month in the Chaco seeing patients. He's there now."

Ted dressed in a clean shirt and trousers. "That means he's probably checking on the general."

"No doubt. It seems we've just missed him, but one of the nursing staff has made an appointment for us. We'll have a consultation with him a week from tomorrow at ten in the morning."

"What's our ailment?"

"We've been in Asunción on business from the States and have come down with some strange symptoms we'd like to discuss with him."

"That's good. It'll give me enough time to fly to Jerusalem on Tuesday and help Deborah gather her things together before we return to Poughkeepsie to set a wedding date."

"What will you tell Deborah when you have to leave again right after that?"

"I'll send for her mother. While I'm away on…business, they can go on a buying spree for the baby. Women love to do things like that."

"I have a feeling Deborah would rather do those things with you."

"Why are you pressing the point?"

"Because you're not acting like an expectant father usually acts."

"What the hell is that supposed to mean?"

"You know exactly what I mean. So far you've shown zero interest in Deborah's condition, and you've never talked about the baby except to acknowledge its existence. You refused to help her pick a name for your child. By now she must've noticed your, shall we say, lack of enthusiasm."

"I'm marrying her, Bernard. What more do you want?"

"I don't want anything. We're talking about Deborah and *her* wants. You shut her out before, with almost disastrous results. Be careful you don't treat your unborn child like our parents treated us, or you'll do irreparable damage."

It took a lot for Bernard to make him angry. "When did you become the expert on child psychology?"

"Correct me if I'm wrong," Bernard mocked, "but I clearly remember both of us receiving our Ph.Ds in childhood misery when our parents ignored us and turned us over to anyone they could bribe to do the parenting for them."

Ted averted his head, not wanting to hear the truth at this particular moment. "I don't feel anything for the baby," he said. "I can't help it."

"That's the way the parents felt about us. Dead inside because of their shame. Look what it did to us, dammit!

"But Deborah will never understand something

like this, especially coming from the kind of home where her parents have shown so much love. For her sake and your child's, you're going to have to try.''

''I'm going to book our flight reservations on the next plane out of here,'' Ted muttered.

''After you do that, let's eat and finish making our plans for the Chaco.''

CHAPTER SIX

"DEBORAH?"

Deborah had heard that voice before.

"Rickie?" she cried out in disbelief. "Are you home from your honeymoon earlier than you'd planned? Was it wonderful?"

How could Rickie have known that Deborah needed to talk to her more than anyone else in the world right now? Ted's sister understood him like no other person. But Deborah hadn't expected to hear from her friend until she'd returned in another week.

"We're still in Tahiti, and I'm so much in love with my husband, I never want our honeymoon to end."

"That's the way love is supposed to be." Deborah swallowed painfully as she considered how far removed she and Ted were from that euphoric state. "What are you doing phoning *me?* You should be with Jordan."

"I've been dying to talk to you, but I received the surprise of my life when your dad answered and told me you'd moved into an apartment with David."

Rickie couldn't know about the wedding yet or she would've said something by now.

Bless Benjamin for leaving it up to Deborah to tell Rickie the news. If Miriam had answered the phone, it would have been a different story.

"That's true, but let's not waste time talking about me. You're supposed to have left the cares of the everyday world behind. You should be giving Jordan your undivided attention."

"He has it. But he's asleep right now."

"What if he wakes up and realizes you're not with him?"

"There's no chance of that. An hour ago he accidentally stepped on a sea urchin while we were out snorkeling. The spines went into the bottom of his foot."

Deborah shuddered. "You're kidding! An ex-Navy SEAL no less. The expert diver?" They both chuckled, then Deborah said on a more serious note, "That must have been horrible!"

"It was. Some of the spines penetrated so deeply that he was in agony. The doctor said they'd eventually come out by themselves. In the meantime, he gave him a painkiller and ordered him to bed with his leg elevated. He's asleep right now."

"Is he going to be all right?"

"Yes. According to the doctor his foot will feel a lot better after twelve hours. Then it'll be more of a nuisance than anything because he'll be hobbling around."

"Somehow I can't picture the great Jordan Browning hobbling, let alone incapacitated."

Rickie's happy laughter floated over the phone line. "To be honest, neither can I. When he wakes up, I guess I'm going to find out what kind of a patient he is."

"For better or worse, eh? If he's grouchy, then I guess you'll just have to come up with some creative ways to keep him entertained," Deborah teased.

Rickie laughed. "Enough about Jordan and me. Deborah, was my plan to bring Ted to his senses a complete failure? I have to know."

She felt a constricting band around her chest. "No. You know your brother amazingly well. A week after the wedding, he broke his silence and proposed for a second time. But—" she said when Rickie would have shouted for joy "—it wasn't for the reasons you suggested."

"What do you mean?" Rickie's suddenly sober tone made Deborah feel guilty for casting any shadows on her friend's happiness. Rickie had been so ecstatic when she first called.

"I don't know what's going on inside him, what drives him. Things aren't the same between us anymore. I'm afraid they never will be again."

"But you're going to marry him because you love him the way I love Jordan...."

Her eyes closed tightly. "Yes," she whispered.

"Thank heaven. I know that deep down Ted loves you."

You told me that once before, but somehow I don't believe it anymore.

"I promise you everything will be all right, Deborah. I promise." Deborah wasn't immune to her friend's emotion and felt tears gather. "How soon are you getting married?" Rickie asked.

"I—I don't know yet." She wiped her eyes. "Ted's due in Jerusalem sometime today. We're going to fly to New York tomorrow to make final plans."

"They'd better include Jordan and me."

"Who else would I have for my matron of honor?"

"Thank you for asking me. Honestly, Deborah, I don't think anything but your wedding could tear me away from here. We've found paradise."

"Before Ted called off our engagement, I felt the same way. I think paradise isn't as much a place as a state of mind."

"And a state of heart," Rickie murmured. "One day you and Ted will experience that kind of joy again. Trust me."

"I have to. Trust is all I've got going for me right now."

"Then you hang on to it. I'll call you at Ted's New York apartment before the weekend. Maybe by then you'll have a date picked out."

"All right. I'm so thankful you called, Rickie."

"Me, too. I always wanted a sister. I love you, Deborah."

"I love you, too."

BEFORE HE LEFT his office to head for the airport, Ted looked over the fax he'd requested from Senator Mason's office.

Confidential
Topic: Senate DNC Probe
Paraguay Link to White House

A Texas businessman, Sunny Gonzales (born in the Antilles and now a legal resident of the U.S.), who was instrumental in raising more than a million dollars for his party, visited the White House at least ten times since July of 1996.

Eight of those ten times, Gonzales met with the president and spent his time lobbying for the president's support of Paraguay's current government to prevent another coup headed by ousted military leader General Oriana.

As early as 1994, the Gonzales Company known as Global Cyber Electronics, had given more than $700,000 to the party and to the presidential and vice presidential campaigns.

The probe has only begun to uncover the facts, but all roads lead to the conclusion that the big donor is attempting to influence U.S. foreign policy in Paraguay.

Secret Service records show that a former White House aide, Clyde Nichols, a major stockholder in the Gonzales Company, first introduced Gonzales to the president.

According to a deposition given by Nichols,

Gonzales does major business in South America, particularly in Paraguay.

Financial records show it would not be in Gonzales's best business interests were the present dictator of Paraguay to be deposed. The matter is still under investigation.

Ted made a copy of the fax, put it in a sealed envelope, then buzzed his secretary. "Alice? I'd like you to personally hand-deliver this to Bernard and no one else. If he's not in his office yet, he will be soon. I'm on my way to Jerusalem. I'll check in with you later."

"Yes, sir."

"Do me another favor, please? Contact Senator Mason's secretary. Find out his preference in champagne. Send it to his office with a basket of fresh fruit and my sincerest compliments."

"Right away. Anything else?"

"Yes. Make sure there are fresh flowers and fruit in the guest suite of my penthouse by tomorrow afternoon."

She smiled. "For Ms. Solomon?"

"Yes. Since you're privy to more information about me than anyone in the entire world, might as well know we're going to be married. But I'd like that kept private until further notice."

"That's wonderful. *She's* wonderful, if you don't mind my saying."

"I don't mind." *How could I mind when she's part of me?*

DEBORAH'S BEAMING MOTHER hurried into the bedroom. "Ted's here."

"I know. I heard the bell."

Actually Deborah had been listening feverishly for his arrival. He'd phoned from the airport and had discovered that she'd come to her parents' house to finish some last-minute packing.

Since they would be living in New York after the wedding, he'd urged her to bring only her clothes and anything she couldn't live without. The rest he would have shipped.

Her mother was still hovering. "He says he has a surprise for both of us."

That sounded like the Ted she'd fallen in love with. During their courtship, he never came empty-handed. Mostly he brought her flowers.

"What do you suppose it could be?" her mother went on.

Deborah shook her head. She knew one thing for sure. Ted was generous to a fault where her parents were concerned. Little gifts arrived for them when they least expected it. An interesting first edition for her father's library, an exotic tortoiseshell comb for her mother's hair.

For a man with billions of dollars, she had to admit he never went overboard or displayed his wealth. Neither did Rickie. If anything, she couldn't give her money away fast enough.

In that regard, the Taylor children had remained remarkably untouched or spoiled by their circumstances. It was just one of the many traits Deborah admired in the man she loved. The man who'd once loved *her*, her heart cried in renewed pain.

"I have no idea, Mom. Tell him I'll be right out."

"Don't keep him waiting," her mother reminded her before disappearing.

This one night, Deborah was determined not to give in to the demons plaguing her. She slid her feet into sandals and glanced at herself in the mirror.

Her chignon was still in place. No slip was showing beneath the loose-fitting yellow sundress that could no longer hide her pregnancy. The modest cotton outfit with its high square neck and broad shoulder straps felt the most comfortable on these hot summer evenings.

Satisfied with her appearance, she left the bedroom and started down the hall. Before she reached the foyer, Ted was there to intercept her.

Her heart began to skid dangerously, and she found breathing difficult. She couldn't blame this reaction on the baby, either—only on Ted.

"Finally!" was all he said before his arms went around her neck and he pulled her against him. His mouth descended on hers, blotting out the world.

He's kissing you like he means it, so pretend he does! There would be time tomorrow to regret this temporary insanity. Tomorrow and all the tomorrows to come.

Dazed by his kiss, she scarcely noticed that he'd followed a silken path down her arms. The next thing she knew, she felt him take her hand and slide something onto the ring finger of her left hand.

On a slight gasp, she broke their kiss long enough to investigate. The same one-carat diamond in the princess cut she liked so much now adorned its former place.

When they'd been dating, Ted had known instinctively that she wouldn't want anything ostentatious. He'd picked out the perfect ring for her.

At the time of their broken engagement, Deborah had been so devastated, she'd torn it from her finger and made Rickie promise to return it to Ted.

The shock of discovering it back on her hand when she'd never expected to see it again made her stagger on her feet.

Ted's grip tightened on her upper arms to support her. "I'll make sure it never comes off again," he vowed before finding her mouth once more.

You say that as if it's going to be a struggle, my darling.

"Deborah?" her mother called. "Ted?"

As he relinquished her mouth, his gaze was so intense his eyes had turned an inky blue. Deborah averted her head. "We're coming, Mom."

As they walked into the living room, his arm lay heavy and possessive around her shoulders. Their hips brushed against each other. *Dear God.* The sensation reminded her of past intimacies and spread like wildfire through her sensitized body.

Before she could say anything, her parents saw the ring sparkling on her finger.

"Ah, there you are. So *that's* the surprise," her mother cried while her father nodded his pleasure at seeing the evidence of their daughter's official engagement.

Ted's mouth curved upward. "I have one more surprise." He reached in the pocket of his chinos for an envelope. Curious, Deborah watched him hand it to her mother.

Miriam opened it and looked up, smiling broadly. "Airline tickets?"

"That's right. If you can arrange it, I've made reservations for you to fly to New York on Thursday and stay until the following Tuesday. That's how long I have to be in England on business. I thought you and Deborah could spend that time buying nursery furniture and things for the baby. You can shop to your heart's content."

While her mother was exclaiming her delight, Deborah heard Ted add, "You're welcome to come too, Ben."

"Thank you, but I think this sounds like a time for my daughter and her mother to be together. That's very generous of you."

Ted couldn't have conceived of a gift that would make her mother happier, but throughout all the banter Deborah fell into a deepening despair. He wasn't even going to be in New York!

He's not happy about the baby. Please God, help him love our son after he's born.

"Now if you'll excuse us." He looked down at Deborah, who fought to keep a pleasant expression on her face. "We have an appointment with your uncle Isaac."

Deborah's eyes widened. "Why?"

"To discuss your *ketubah.*"

Her father's eyes twinkled. "I see you know about that already."

"A man contemplating marriage needs to see his path clearly before him."

"Amen," her father murmured as the two of them exchanged private smiles.

The *ketubah,* was the Jewish marriage contract, recorded in Aramaic, and outlined the financial and moral obligations the husband was prepared to take on for his wife, to protect her in the marriage.

A shudder passed through Deborah's body. Ted could joke about such matters, but she knew he was deadly earnest about his promise to be a good husband to her.

Love didn't prompt this outward display of devotion and respect. Ted was determined to do his duty. So far he was performing it admirably. She could find no fault. She felt as if she'd been abandoned a second time.

Perhaps because of her silence, Ted unexpectedly brushed her cheek with his lips and whispered, "In case anything happened to me, even before our ceremony took place, I'd want you and the baby provided for."

In case anything happened?

Her heart jumped into her throat.

Like what?

He wasn't dying, was he?

She started to feel light-headed.

Was that what this was all about? Had he tried to spare her the anguish by pretending not to be in love with her anymore?

Oh no, please God, no!

She couldn't suppress an anguished groan. Everyone reacted at once.

"Deborah!" Ted's cry of alarm sounded a hundred-percent genuine. Her parents moved toward her, arms reaching out.

"I—I'm sorry." She bent over and pressed her hand against her stomach. "The baby moved in a way he's never moved before. I'll be all right. Excuse me for a minute while I go to my room."

I need to think.

I'm going to call Bernard.

Ted's features looked bleak. "I'm phoning your doctor. Do you have the number, Miriam?"

Deborah put a detaining hand on his arm. "No, Ted! Don't do that. This isn't serious. The doctor told me I would experience strange aches and pains throughout the pregnancy. If it happens again, then I'll call."

The tension was explosive.

"I want your word on that," he demanded with a ferocity she hadn't witnessed before.

"I promise."

On the way to her room, she heard her mother suggest they sit down in the living room and enjoy a cup of coffee while they waited.

As soon as Deborah was alone and had shut the door, she found the little address book in her purse.

There were three numbers for Bernard. She phoned his condo and got his voice mail but didn't want to leave a message. She tried his cellular phone and got through right away.

"Bernard?"

"Deborah? Where are you? Isn't Ted with you?"

"Yes. We're at my parents' house," she said in hushed tones.

"Why are you calling me? Is something wrong?"

She swallowed hard. "I don't know, and I don't have long to talk."

After a hesitation, he asked, "What's going on?"

"That's what I'd like to know." Her fingers twisted in the telephone cord. "This is one time you have to be honest with me."

"Of course."

"There's no 'of course' about it." Fear and anger had replaced normal civility. "You've kept silent all these months out of loyalty to Ted. But if he has a terminal illness, I think I have a right to know."

"*What?*"

"You heard me, so don't pretend you didn't." She knew she was out of control but couldn't seem to help it. "Is he going to die? Is that why he wrote me that letter, thinking he'd spare me? If you have even one ounce of compassion left for me, then you'll tell me the truth. Otherwise I'm phoning Rickie and Ted's parents for answers."

"I'm not dying," a familiar voice said behind her.

Ted! She hadn't heard him come into her bedroom. He took the receiver out of her hands.

"Bernard? I'll call you later."

She stayed where she was on the edge of the bed. In truth, she was glad he'd followed her to the bedroom. Because he'd listened in on her conversation with Bernard, she could finally bring everything out in the open.

"I won't apologize for phoning your cousin, although in hindsight I realize he'd never reveal your secret any more than you would."

"There is no secret, darling. What I don't understand is how in a matter of seconds, your mind jumped from the mention of a simple wedding formality to my death."

"Stop it, Ted! This is the only thing that's made sense to me since the day you…you destroyed my world."

His eyes darkened. He didn't like being reminded of his cruelty.

"Anyone knowing our situation would agree that a fatal illness would explain that letter you sent me, when you *suddenly* decided you'd fallen out of love with me. It would account for your weight loss, the shadows under your eyes.

"It would explain why you haven't asked me about my pregnancy or shown the slightest interest in the baby. It explains your desire to do your duty for the child you never wanted."

He stood there with his arms folded across his chest, his expression inscrutable. "You're wrong, Deborah. There's only one reason I broke off with you."

"You mean so I could find a nice Jewish boy to marry instead? One who wouldn't impede my devotion to God? You thought I believed that?" she scoffed. "David certainly didn't. I'm quite sure my parents didn't, either, but they love you so much—" Her voice wobbled. "They love you so much they were willing to suspend their disbelief to see me taken care of and accept you into the family."

"That love goes both ways," came his quiet reassurance. "As for convincing you that I'm not lying about the perfect state of my health, I guess I'll have to go on living to prove that to you."

Defeated by this pointless conversation, she got up from the bed. There'd be no answers tonight or any other night.

"If by chance you're telling the truth about not being ill," she began in a low voice, "then you're involved with another woman."

He recoiled.

Did I finally hit upon the truth?

"It's all right, Ted. I've been dealing with that possibility since I read your letter. I can handle it as long as you don't flaunt her in my face. Of course after the baby's born, I expect you to be discreet. The one thing I won't tolerate is his life being blighted by gossip about the latest woman to catch your eye."

"What woman would that be?" He sounded angry.

"I hit a nerve, did I? But to get back to the point—this woman, whoever she is, reminded you how awful it would be to get trapped in a marriage you didn't want.

"You know what people say. Engagements were established to help both parties find out before it's too late if a lifetime together is what they truly want."

She reached for her purse. "Let's get this visit to Uncle Isaac's over with, shall we?"

TED SAW the blinking light on the bedside phone when he walked into his hotel room at the Jerusalem Towers. In his haste to get to Deborah's house earlier that evening and put the engagement ring back on her finger, he'd forgotten to take his cell phone with him.

He hoped the light meant Bernard had been trying to reach him, but he feared it might be Deborah.

In the half hour since he'd driven her home from her uncle's in his rental car, it was possible she'd changed her mind about marrying him. Once he'd seen her safely inside the house, she couldn't say good-night to him fast enough.

He'd left in a state of mental and emotional turmoil, knowing that if he'd attempted to touch her, he would have alienated her even more. Taking that risk now could only deepen the rift he'd created when he'd broken her heart.

Deborah loved him. No man had ever been given greater proof. She loved him with the same depth of love he felt for her.

Seeing her agony tonight because she thought he

might be dying had increased his guilt. Listening to her in the bedroom as she'd tried to build a case of infidelity against him to explain his behavior was haunting him in new ways.

Except for obeying the amenities of politeness in front of her uncle, Deborah had let the men do all the talking. She'd barely listened. On the drive back to her parents', the car might as well have been a tomb for all the life or animation she exhibited. At this rate, it wouldn't be long before her love turned to something else. Resentment or bitterness or even hatred. Maybe the process had already begun.

But it was still better that she despise him for her erroneous imaginings than learn his real identity.

He checked the message—it *was* from Bernard—then drank a bottle of mineral water and phoned him back.

"You know what I think?" his cousin started in the second he heard Ted's voice. "She's in so much pain, the truth couldn't be any worse."

Ted's head fell back against the pillow. He closed his eyes. "First Rickie deserted me. *Et tu, Brute?*"

"You may lose Deborah before we find von Haase and bring him in."

"That's been the risk from the start. What did you think of the fax I had sent over?"

"When Arbizu tells Oriana that our offer's going to make Sunny Gonzalez's fund for the opposition look like so much chicken feed, we'll be given the run of the compound."

"My thoughts exactly. You realize that in getting

what we want, we may also be giving Paraguay a new dictator.''

"I won't lose any sleep over it. Oriana won't be any worse or any better than the current head.''

"According to John Mason, the majority of Congress agrees with you. That's off the record, of course. When there's a Senate probe to discover why Global Banking suddenly has interests in Paraguay, we'll testify that we're running a pilot program of user-friendly ATM machines. That will be the end of the story.''

"We'd better cover our bases by setting things up in Argentina and Chile first.''

"I was just coming to that. Since you know who to contact for those arrangements, why don't you get started on that tomorrow? Until we leave for Asunción on Sunday, I'm going to be busy planning my wedding.''

"How can I help?''

The question was so typical of Bernard, Ted was humbled by it. "You already have. In case you didn't know, I couldn't have made it through life without you.''

"That's funny because I was just going to tell you the same thing. Talk to you later.''

"Good night…''

CHAPTER SEVEN

TED STOOD in the middle of the his living room, their luggage still sitting on the Oriental rug. Moments before, Deborah had disappeared into the guest bedroom after another tense exchange.

Out of concern for her welfare, he'd suggested she lie down for a while because he realized the flight had been tiring for her. He assumed she'd be happy for the respite.

But he'd said the wrong thing. Though careful not to accuse him, she'd implied that she understood why he wanted his privacy. Then she'd walked out on him. He couldn't allow the situation to continue.

When he opened her bedroom door, he was at least pleased to see that his wishes had been carried out. A large shocking-pink azalea, Deborah's favorite flower, sat on the dresser and brought life to the dove-gray-and-white decor. On the bedside table, he saw a basket brimming with bananas, apples and pears, in case she got hungry.

She had gone into the attached bathroom. He sat down in one of the side chairs and waited.

To his chagrin, she seemed startled when she came out and found him in her room. Her nervousness wounded him. Their relationship had degenerated so totally from the way things once were, he realized he'd need to court her all over again if they were going to recover even a fraction of their former happiness.

"What do you want?" Her beautiful brown eyes had lost their luster. Something else he had to feel guilty about... "Did the rabbi change our appointment?"

"No. It's still arranged for tomorrow afternoon. Until then, I thought you and I might use the time to look for a house."

The stunned expression on her face meant he'd caught her off guard. Gratified by that much reaction, he said, "I've been thinking about the baby. Until you told me you were pregnant, I never felt the need to move from the penthouse. Over the years it's served me well.

"But I'm a family man now. Except for a piece of paper making it official, you're already my wife, and we have a baby on the way.

"There are dozens of charming homes on quiet streets in and around Poughkeepsie. The thought of having to use the elevator every day to take our son for a ride in his stroller along a busy city street sounds preposterous. What I'd like us to find is a cozy place of our own with a yard."

"When you mean 'cozy,' are you thinking of a fifty-room house with servants' quarters?"

The acerbic question sounded out of character for Deborah. A second later, he heard her say, "I—I'm sorry. No matter what's happened between us, that comment was uncalled for. Neither you nor Rickie has ever made it a secret that you hated living at Graycliff.''

I love you, Deborah. But if I were to tell you that right now, and act on those feelings, I would lose the little bit of ground I've just gained.

''Apology accepted. Does the idea of buying a home appeal to you?''

Color filled her cheeks. ''Of course it does.'' She fiddled with her hands. How long had it been since he'd felt them on his body? Touching him. Loving him.

Abruptly he returned his thoughts to their conversation. ''Then it's settled. I'll call Mark in our real estate department and have him pull up the latest listing of homes in Dutchess County. We can drive around today and tomorrow until we see a few places that really appeal from the outside.

''Then we'll have him give us the indoor tours. All we have to do is pick out the one that suits us best, and we'll start the paperwork.''

''You really want to go looking right now?''

At the slight tremor in her voice, he had to stifle a moan. She was as vulnerable as hell. He was the one who'd made her this way.

He got up from the chair and came to stand in front of her.

''Until Sunday morning, when I have to go out of town on business for a couple of days, I'm all yours.'' He cupped her hot cheeks in his hands. ''I wouldn't want to be anywhere else, nor with anyone else," he whispered against her lips before tasting the mouth he'd been craving.

She didn't fight him, thank God.

DON'T KISS ME like this, Ted. Please don't— I lose all sense of time and place, of right and wrong. This is wrong. But the minute you touch me, I dissolve. I forget you didn't want to marry me. I forget that the baby is the only reason I'm standing in your home right now, kissing you as if my life depended on it. It does *depend on it.*

Finding some hidden reserve of strength, she managed to pull away from him first. In that instant before there was space between them, she saw the familiar glaze of passion in his eyes.

He might be involved with another woman, but it was a balm to Deborah's open wounds to know that he could still feel desire for *her.*

At least that hadn't gone yet.

She'd thought she wanted it gone. She'd thought that what he'd done to her had burned out every bit of feeling. She'd thought she didn't care if they became roommates instead of lovers.

She'd been wrong.

Instead of just standing there so close he could hear her shallow breathing, why didn't he say something? Do something?

She knew why. He was waiting for her to decide whether they'd go out looking at houses or go to bed. The choice was up to her. He'd never forced her and never would. He wasn't that kind of man.

They'd made love too many times for her not to know that he always put her pleasure ahead of his. In fact, he would've been willing to wait until their wedding night to make love if that had been her desire.

Something must be wrong with her that she could stand here like this defending his virtues when he'd done his best to murder her heart.

Could she make it through their travesty of a marriage like this? With the trust gone? With her heart damaged, her feelings numb?

The physical bond between them was still intact. The real question was whether they could achieve any kind of emotional harmony, let alone peace.

With her feelings still too raw, she took the definitive step away from him. "If Mother's going to help us outfit a nursery, I think we'd better start our search for a house."

"I'll phone Mark."

Ted's level response displayed no emotion either way, but before he pulled out his cellular phone, she detected the little nerve that sometimes throbbed in his jaw when he was under stress.

It meant her decision had disappointed him. She knew a moment's rejoicing that she had any power over his feelings, insignificant and temporary as that power might be.

His conversation with Mark didn't last long. He put the phone back in his pocket. "Maybe you'd better use the bathroom one more time while I go into the study and get the list he's faxing. It might be a good idea to grab a piece of fruit in case you get a sudden urge for something. Then we'll be off.''

His comment brought the first smile to her lips in days. So far she hadn't experienced those wild cravings for food she'd always heard about. But the urge to throw herself into his arms was growing into a need she'd have to do something about if they didn't leave soon.

Maybe the suggestion that they go house-hunting had been a calculated move on his part to dispel some of the ugliness of that awful scene in her bedroom the day before. Whatever his motives, she wasn't unhappy about it.

Ted's penthouse was a glorified bachelor's condo, tastefully equipped for a man who, along with his cousin, was second in command of a huge empire. Transforming one of the guest bedrooms into a nursery wouldn't make the place a real home.

Long before she'd met Ted, Deborah, like all her girlfriends, had talked and dreamed of living in a beautiful home one day with the man she loved, of raising a beautiful family.

She hadn't thought of that home in terms of size or particular furnishings. It was more of a *feeling*.

Like the warmth that entered her heart when she thought of her parents' home. Delicious smells wafting from the oven. The comforting sound of her mother's cajoling, her father's gentle teasing, their laughter. David's off-key humming. All of it a haven of security and love.

A sudden fierce desire to create that kind of home for Ted and their baby welled up inside her. Ted couldn't talk about his home or his childhood. He adored Rickie and Bernard, of course. But despite his great wealth, the fabulous estate he'd grown up on, he'd never known the richness of family life.

She could try to create a sense of family for him, or at least attempt it. She would do it anyway for her son. She needed a worthy goal, a purpose. Why not this one?

Perhaps, in the striving, Ted would enter into the spirit of things. Maybe after he returned from his trip to England next Tuesday, he would talk to her again with openness and honesty and tell her what had caused him to deliberately destroy something as wonderful as their love.

THE OUTPATIENT department at Government Hospital looked overcrowded and understaffed. Their appointment had been set for ten o'clock. At 11:40 a.m., a nurse called Bernard's name. He and Ted followed the woman to a cubicle at the far end of the hall.

She put some papers on the desk and told them to sit down. After pulling the curtain to give them privacy, she left them alone. Bernard perched on the examining table, Ted on the wooden chair.

A slight silver-haired man wearing steel-rimmed bifocals bustled into the cubicle. He had to be in his mid- to late sixties. His face showed a mixture of Indian and Spanish blood.

"Buenos días, señores."

"Good morning," Bernard answered. "Do you speak English?"

"Of course. Most tourists get angry when we try to speak English with them, so I always start out in Spanish."

Ted chuckled. He liked the doctor's humor.

Dr. Arbizu studied them with a keen eye. "I understand you are both suffering from the same sickness. Tell me your symptoms."

Bernard put a finger to the other man's thin lips. "We're not sick," he whispered. "We want you to arrange a meeting for us with General Oriana at his headquarters in Stroessnerplatz."

Ted added, in the same low voice, "It's very unfortunate that his coup failed several years ago, largely because of Sunny Gonzalez's contributions to the prevailing political party to back your current president."

By this time the doctor's body had gone rigid. He removed his glasses and started a dexterous cleaning of them with a fresh tissue.

"We're aware Oriana is planning to stage another coup. But that kind of takeover costs money," Ted continued. "We're businessmen who'd like to offer our financial support. Naturally, we'll want some favors in return...."

"We do not deal in drugs. No black market. Everything is legitimate. Since you're his doctor, we're counting on you to convey our message."

Bernard pulled a bundled wad of bills from his

briefcase. "This is for you. Ten thousand American dollars' worth of guaraníes for your trouble. If you don't wish to help us, then keep the money or give it to your favorite charity."

"This—" Ted indicated the rest "—represents one hundred thousand American dollars for the general. All the bills are unmarked. Take this to him. Tell him this is only a fraction of what could be available if he's interested. If he's not, tell him to keep the money and use it to outfit his army."

The doctor put his glasses back on. "Gentlemen—you cannot possibly be serious. I do not know what you are talking about. I've never heard of a General Oriana."

"Of course you have. You travel to the Chaco every month. You've been seen entering Stroessnerplatz many times to tend to the wounds he received during his last coup attempt." *Maybe you're von Haase's physician, as well.* "You wouldn't have lived this long to practice medicine if you didn't have the general's confidence."

"You can contact us at ten o'clock tonight at this number with his answer." Bernard handed him a piece of paper with an untraceable cell phone number they'd had set up for this operation inside Paraguay. "How much for today's visit?"

The good doctor looked on the verge of apoplexy. "T-twenty American dollars each."

"Where do we pay?"

"At the cashier outside the double doors of the outpatient department."

"Mark the treatment on the forms and sign them so we can leave."

Ted could see the man's hands were shaking as he wrote his signature on both papers.

Bernard took them. "Thank you, Doctor. Have a good day."

As they left the cubicle, Ted glanced back and realized Arbizu was terrified. He could commiserate with him. Arbizu knew very well that in a country like Paraguay, being presented with that kind of money meant the donors were rich, powerful—and deadly if crossed.

A few minutes later they were once again ensconced in a taxi headed for a different hotel than the one they'd used the previous week.

"Is there any question in your mind that we'll be getting a phone call tonight?" Bernard whispered.

Ted shook his head. "We were right to give him a hundred thousand. Oriana will know we wouldn't hand over that kind of money if we weren't talking major bucks. Under the circumstances he's not going to shoot the messenger."

"I WANT TO BUY everything in the store!"

Deborah could only echo her mother's sentiments. No wonder Ted had suggested this would be a good place to come. The Baby Swiss Shop carried such unique and beautiful handcrafted things from Switzerland, she didn't see how she'd ever be able to make a decision.

"Oh! Will you look at the hand-painted cradle

with all those hearts and the little canopy with the lace! I suppose it would be all right to put a boy in it.''

"I don't think so, Mom. This is the girls' section. Let's walk over to the other side of the store.''

Her mother had also wanted to buy everything in the last store, where they'd picked out blankets and sleepers and crib sheets that were going to be delivered at a later date.

"You would've looked so beautiful in that cradle. I want to buy it so you'll have it for your baby girl someday.''

Deborah rubbed her temples where an ache had started. She'd known this would happen once they began looking at baby furniture. Her father had known it, too, and had wisely remained in Jerusalem with David. Already her mother was envisioning the future with her grandchildren, and Deborah wasn't even married yet.

The ceremony wouldn't be for ten more days. Ted had wanted it sooner, but Deborah insisted they wait for Rickie and Jordan to get home from their honeymoon. It hurt Deborah that Ted wasn't on the friendliest terms with his sister. That was another subject he didn't want to talk about.

Right now, Deborah's life with him was so precarious, she couldn't see past the next twenty-four hours. That was when Ted and Bernard were due home from their business trip. Then she and Ted would decide which house to buy. The choice had been narrowed down to two that Deborah liked.

Her mother was still chatting excitedly about future grandchildren when Deborah interrupted. "Let's concentrate on the baby I'm carrying, Mom."

They wandered from one display to another, then cried out at the same time when they saw the three-piece grouping in a corner of the boys' department. It consisted of a classically designed crib, dresser and rocking chair in a sky-blue finish, all trimmed with little hand-painted farm animals with the dearest faces.

"This is it! If only your fiancé were here to see it!"

Deborah walked over to the dresser and tried one of the drawers. It opened and closed with the smooth precision of all Swiss-made things. "I have to admit I love it, too."

She didn't believe the color of Ted's eyes had anything to do with her choice. As far as she was concerned, this set looked like something you saw in a children's picture book. It suggested home and warmth and love—everything she wanted to surround her baby with.

"Ted has such wonderful taste. He knew we'd find the perfect thing for my grandson in here."

Ted was pretty perfect in her mother's eyes.

He's pretty perfect to me, too. Damn him for making me fall in love with him! Damn him for his secrets.

"I'll tell the saleslady we want it. Then we can go back to the penthouse. I'm exhausted."

"Of course you are. I'll fix us some dinner, and after that we'll call your father and David."

Deborah nodded in relief. She'd go to bed early, she decided. All day, she'd been trying not to hope Ted would phone. She'd been trying not to miss him. But that hadn't worked, either. Three days seemed like three weeks. She couldn't stop thinking about him. It was all starting again. The aching, the wanting, the needing. She'd sworn she wasn't going to do this....

"DEBORAH?"

"Ted! Where are you?"

She had missed him. He could tell by the way her voice caught when she said his name. He'd missed her, too. Desperately.

"I'm on my way in from the airport. I should be there in five minutes. Did your mother get off all right this morning?"

"Yes. She called a little while ago to let me know she's home safely."

"That's good. How did the shopping go?"

"You'll find out when you get the bills. Let me say hello to Bernard."

Maybe he was dreaming, but she sounded like the old Deborah. He dreaded saying anything that might change the warmth in her voice.

"You're too late. The taxi just dropped him off at his condo."

"Then I'll talk to him tomorrow. Was your trip successful?"

Ted was still elated. Oriana swallowed the bait. The meeting at Stroessnerplatz would take place in three weeks' time.

He forced himself to sound matter-of-fact. "In a manner of speaking, but conferences can be dull. I'm glad to be home."

When there was silence, he realized it would be too much to expect Deborah to admit she was glad, too.

"Are you hungry?"

"No. I ate on the plane." *All I want is to take you to bed with me.*

"Have you had dinner?"

"Yes. Mother made herself at home in your kitchen. We have enough food to last several meals."

"If she happened to make my favorite bread, then I'm still hungry."

"I'll tell her you said that. It'll make her day."

"Listen, the taxi's pulling up to the curb. I'll be with you in a minute."

He paid the driver and hurried into the foyer with his carry-on bag. Before he entered the elevator, he removed the tag from the handle and pulled his airline stubs from his pocket. Then he tossed everything in the waste bin. That way, there'd be no evidence of where he'd been. No evidence for *her* to find.

The ride to the penthouse seemed to take too long. *Come on.*

Finally the door slid open.

"Deborah?"

He should have known she wouldn't be there to greet him. Disappointment hit him hard as he set down his bag and went in search of her. "Where are you?"

"In the dining room. I've got both floor plans spread out on the table. Come and look."

She had houses on her mind. He had something else. She could have no idea how much he needed her tonight.

"Have you decided which house you want?"

"I think so, but I'm waiting to see if it's the same one you choose."

When he walked into the room she looked up, but her gaze didn't welcome him as much as it appeared to study him. It was possible she would never trust him again.

She gestured to the plans but he couldn't see anything except her. The sleeveless, lightweight dress in shades of brown and bronze brought out the sheen of her lustrous dark eyes. Her hair had been formed into its usual braid and hung over her shoulder. She looked soft and golden.

"Do you feel as good as you look?" He closed the distance between them and bestowed a quick kiss to her lips.

"I'm fine, thanks, but you seem a little tired. You'd never admit it but you work too hard."

Those weren't exactly the words he wanted to hear. Still, they could be construed as having a wifely ring. He supposed that was something to cherish.

"I'm not working now."

In an effort to counteract her power over him, he continued through to the kitchen. At least he could satisfy one of his appetites, he thought as he broke off a chunk of her mother's bread. It was sweet to the taste with a cakelike texture he found irresistible. He could never get enough of it.

Deborah affected him the same way.

He pulled a cold cola from the refrigerator and returned to the other room. "All right." He took a long swallow. "Let me see those plans and I'll tell you what I think."

Still wanting contact, he stood behind her chair. The scent of her skin made him feel almost faint. He put his drink on the table and slid his hands over her shoulders. It was a struggle to keep his eyes on the layouts rather than the voluptuous lines of her body.

"The best thing to recommend them is that they're the antithesis of Graycliff," he said. "Both houses are in good residential neighborhoods in Poughkeepsie Town. Lots of younger couples with children. Schools and parks nearby.

"They're both in the Cape style we like, with dormer windows and cathedral ceilings in the family rooms. Three bedrooms upstairs, any one of which will make an attractive nursery," he continued, re-viewing their qualities in a businesslike tone.

"A sunroom, dining room, large open kitchen and living room with fireplace downstairs. Laundry rooms, three baths. Three-thousand square feet of cozy house surrounded by yards that could be fenced to hold a little boy and his dog."

He felt the tremor that passed through her body. Those words had pleased her.

"I think I choose this one." He released her shoulder long enough to tap the plan on the right.

"That's the one I picked." She sounded out of breath. "The den and living room are at the front of the house. I like that arrangement better. Then, if the kitchen and family room are a little messy, unexpected guests won't realize it."

"Are you a messy housekeeper, my love?" He kissed the side of her neck.

"Well, I know I'm not as meticulous as my mother."

He found a certain sensitive spot at the nape. "Much as I love your mother, it's you I'm marrying. You know, I like the thought of a house that's lived in.

"Graycliff was an enormous museum, always on display, not a piece of period furniture out of place. Cooks, maids, housekeepers, gardeners, all kinds of people employed to keep its wheels well-oiled. You have my permission to be as messy as you want. I'll help."

She laughed out loud. He hadn't heard such a spontaneous sound in a long time. It was music to his ears.

He picked up his drink and finished it off.

"I—I love the house, Ted. Thank you for your

generosity. How soon do you think we can move in?''

"After our honeymoon."

In a sudden jerky movement, she turned in the chair. "Panic" was the only way to describe her expression. It hurt him all over again, because he realized how much she'd changed from the eager woman who couldn't wait for all that love had in store for them.

Like ripples across a still pond, the effects of the damage he'd inflicted would continue to follow him.

"On the other hand," he said, "since you'll be in your third trimester then, maybe it would be wisest to postpone it."

We don't have to go on a honeymoon to make love. It's what I intend to do, what I'm waiting to do once we say our vows.

She moistened her lips in a telltale sign of nervousness. "Thank you for understanding. To be honest, I'm so excited about the house, I'd rather stay here and get settled in. Wait till you see the furniture for the baby's room!"

A new light entered her eyes every time she mentioned the baby.

If that reaction had happened because of her interest in another man, he couldn't have felt any more jealous.

Soon, my darling, when you're back in my bed, your eyes will light up that same way for me.

CHAPTER EIGHT

"SHOW HER the bottom of your foot, darling," Rickie urged.

Jordan grinned at Deborah. With his green eyes and black hair that had grown longer and curlier in the last month, he was as handsome as Ted in his own right. "You're sure you want to see this?"

Deborah smiled back, staring at the bronzed couple who were so in love, they radiated their happiness to everyone around them. A pain shot through Deborah's heart when she remembered that she and Ted had once been like that.

"I've never seen a sea urchin, let alone its spines. Since I'm not a good swimmer, this is probably the closest I'll ever come to the experience."

"Are you ready for this, Mary?"

Mary Moe, a relative of Stoney's, helped run the office of his and Jordan's legitimate air cargo company.

Only a select few people knew the growing charter business fronted their illegal operation to airlift the endangered Aché Indians from the Paraguayan Chaco. The compound became their new shelter and a place to learn the life skills they'd need to be self-sufficient in western society.

The Quonset style huts left over from World War II had been remodeled on the inside, for business and personal use. Outwardly, however, the vintage buildings didn't draw that much attention from the community. Jordan and Stoney wanted to keep things that way.

As for Mary, she was pure gold. Not only was she a loving mother to the Indian families who needed her constant nurturing, her amusing personality and down-to-earth humor would throw off even the most suspicious person snooping around the premises.

Right now, she was quite a sight as she leaned her head of orangeish-red hair as far over the counter as she could. She was wearing two orchid leis Rickie and Jordan had brought her back from Tahiti. They'd put a couple of leis around Deborah's neck, as well.

"I've been waiting a long time for this moment, honey. Let's see what you got!"

Jordan threw back his head and laughed. "Don't say I didn't warn you." He lifted his long, hard-muscled leg and propped it on the magazine table. Rickie removed the sock.

"Holy Toledo!" Mary bellowed. "Do all those little holes mean the spines are still in there?"

"The tips of them anyway," Rickie explained. "They're slowly dissolving."

Deborah shook her head. "That must have been awful."

She saw the private look that passed between Jor-

dan and his wife before he said, "Awful. I had to
stay in bed for a whole week."

Mary's all-knowing eyes zeroed in on Rickie.
"According to my calculations, that means I'm going to be a grandma in about eight months."

"Those are some calculations, Mary," Jordan
muttered out of the side of his mouth.

Rickie was too tanned for the blush to show, but
Deborah knew it was there, flowing up her neck and
into her cheeks.

Maybe Mary's words were prophetic. Deborah
hoped they were. She couldn't imagine anything
more wonderful than her sister-in-law having a baby
right away. Ted's relationship with his cousin, Bernard, had meant so much to him during their childhood; it still did. She wanted the same kind of closeness for her own son.

Mary's eyes suddenly darted to Deborah. "And
to think I'm going to be an aunt in a few months.
That ought to get me into practice for your big
event, Jordan."

Jordan chuckled again. Everyone loved Mary's
warmth and generosity, her enthusiasm; Deborah
was no different in that regard. "I'm so glad you're
coming to the wedding tomorrow."

She cocked her head. "It's going to be a Jewish
wedding, right? Where you all sing 'Hava' something and everyone throws their wineglasses? Or is
that from some other kind of wedding?"

"I think that's a Greek tradition," Jordan said,
smiling.

"You're partially correct, Mary," Deborah explained. "There is a glass involved. The groom crushes it with his foot. Ted's looking forward to that part, too."

"Well, it sounds fun. Do the guests have to say anything?" she sounded anxious. "I'm having enough trouble learning Guaraní."

Now Deborah was laughing. "No."

Jordan put a loving arm around Rickie, who smiled up at her husband and said, "The only words will have to come from Ted and Deborah when they say, 'I do.'"

Deborah glanced away in pain. She would give anything to be as happy as the two of them, to be that free to tease her husband, to joke with him, to share private memories. No shadows, no secrets. No fears that she wasn't loved by the man she'd married.

"Come on, Deborah." Rickie unexpectedly took her arm. "I'll walk you out to your car. I can't believe you took time on the day before your wedding to drive out to the hangar and welcome us home."

"We're all looking forward to tomorrow," Jordan assured her. "Stoney and Michelle will be there, too. We'll get to the synagogue early in case there's some last-minute thing we can do to help. Give our best to Ted."

She felt a lump in her throat at their outpouring of love. No one knew how much she needed the support just then. "I will. Thank you all. I'll see you later."

Neither she nor Rickie spoke until they reached the white Honda Civic Ted had bought Deborah yesterday. He'd insisted she needed a car, and they'd gone looking at several brands. Always practical, she'd chosen the Honda because it got good mileage and moved in and out of traffic easily.

He'd done so much for her already—bought her a house and a car, everything he thought she might need. But the only gift she truly wanted was the one he couldn't give.

"I take it things aren't going that well." Rickie spoke first.

Deborah let out a shuddering sigh. "Everything's perfect except for one thing."

She felt Rickie put a comforting arm around her shoulders. "Don't ever give up hope. Promise me you won't. Whatever haunts him, it doesn't have anything to do with you. You're the woman he fell in love with. That hasn't changed."

"But it changes my ability to respond to him!"

"Deborah—"

The empathy in Rickie's tone didn't help the painful state of Deborah's emotions.

"I *want* to respond," she cried out. "What I want, more than anything, is for us to be together the way we once were. But the fact remains, we wouldn't be getting married if it weren't for the baby. My mind won't let me forget that, even if my heart's willing not to look back." She threw her arms around Rickie in a quick hug. "Now I've got to go."

"We've kept you too long. Ted's probably going out of his mind wondering where you are."

She shook her head. "No. Bernard and the guys at the office are giving him a bachelor party. I'm sorry they didn't include Jordan. I don't understand why."

"Don't worry about it. Ted and I have always been so close, I'm afraid he had a hard time seeing me get married. I think he views Jordan as the man who took me away from him. It'll pass."

"I'm sure it will. He adores you."

"So, what are you going to do with your last night of freedom?"

Deborah made a face. "Don't I wish. I'll be staying at the Dutchess Inn with my family. Everyone's here. Mom, Dad, David, three aunts and uncles, five cousins. My aunts refuse to let me see Ted before the wedding tomorrow."

"You're lucky to be surrounded by so many loving relatives," Rickie murmured. Whenever she or Ted talked about their own family, there was always a sad, wistful sound in Rickie's voice, a hollowness in Ted's. It saddened Deborah more than she could say.

"I wish I could invite your parents, but Ted won't hear of it."

"No. But I'll tell them you wanted to. I know they'd like to meet you. Maybe after the baby's born."

Deborah nodded. "Thank you, my dear friend.

Just think. Tomorrow night we'll be sisters."

"I can't wait!"

EARLY MONDAY EVENING, Ted hurried into the Mid-Hudson Valley Temple, a synagogue designed along classic New England lines. In his opinion, the interior's most interesting feature was the design of the ark, which contained four Torahs, one of which was more than two hundred years old.

"Rabbi Arnavitz? Forgive me for being late, especially when I'm the one who requested this meeting. I didn't realize my secretary had arranged for a surprise toast before I left work. Since she'd gone to the trouble, I couldn't in all decency break away until now."

"Of course not." The graying, slim, sixty-year-old rabbi shook Ted's hand, then invited him to sit down opposite his desk. "You've been diligent in keeping your appointments. I commend you for taking your commitments seriously. If there'd been a problem, I knew you would have phoned me."

"Thank you." More and more Ted was warming to the man.

"When Deborah informed me that she didn't feel a rehearsal was necessary due to the small, intimate nature of your wedding, I wondered if you might not have a few last-minute questions."

"Not in the sense you're thinking, but there is something that's bothering me."

"Go on."

"We've been over this ground before. Deborah is giving up a lot to marry me. In her desire to simplify the ceremony—to make this experience easier for all of us—I'm afraid she may have left out something truly important to her."

"Your concern is a credit to you, but I can assure you that all the necessary elements will be incorporated."

"Maybe. But she refused to consider a big celebration with a band and dancing. She and I attended one in Jerusalem, and I could tell she wanted that same kind of wedding for herself. This won't be like anything she'd once envisioned."

"Perhaps because of her pregnancy and the fact that your wedding party is confined to family members and a few close friends, she feels more comfortable with a simple catered dinner in our social hall afterward."

Ted's brows knit in a frown.

"That's probably true." But deep inside he knew the real reason she'd taken no joy in the wedding preparations. He'd robbed her of what ought to be the happiest day of her life. He wanted to make up for that in whatever way he could. "Tell me, Rabbi. Is there anything I can do tomorrow to make the ceremony a little more personal for her?"

"What kind of thing do you mean?"

"So far, she's planned all the elements of the ceremony with you, which is as it should be. This is all pretty unfamiliar to me, so it wasn't my place to get involved in the arrangements.

"However, I find that I'd like to add my contribution. Something private and…unexpected, if you will. I love her deeply and would like to show her that this marriage is every bit as sacred to me.''

The rabbi had been sitting back in his swivel chair, palms joined together in front of his lips. By the time Ted had finished speaking, he nodded and sat forward.

''There are several things you can do. And your bride will know the deep significance of each one and be thrilled that you bothered to learn them to please her.''

Ted's heart kicked over. ''That's perfect! Exactly what I'm talking about. Give me an example.''

A smile broke the corner of the rabbi's mouth. ''Here's something you can do before the wedding ceremony.''

David nodded eagerly.

''Once you've both dressed in your wedding finery, and you have a moment alone, lift the tip of her veil with one hand and peek underneath it.''

''What is the significance?''

''To see if it's really Deborah. The gesture is symbolic of Jacob looking to see if he's got Rachel or Leah.''

''I like that,'' Ted said with a smile. ''Tell me more.''

''During the ceremony the two of you will be standing in front of me. Your bride won't be expecting any physical contact, but in some ceremonies I've witnessed, the couple holds hands—or even embrace. You could do that if you prefer.''

''I do prefer.''

The rabbi winked. "I thought you might. Now about the rings. Deborah has indicated she'll wear them on her left hand, as is traditional in the States.

"When you go through *kiddushin,* which I've explained is the betrothal part of the ceremony, you can surprise her by placing the wedding band on her right hand, as is Jewish custom, before reciting the marriage formula. To make the moment even more moving and personal for her, you could give her a ring that has always belonged to you. She'll be expecting the wedding band you bought with her engagement ring."

Ted remembered a silver ring with fine etching he'd purchased in Toledo, Spain, years ago. He hadn't worn it in ages. If he could get it sized in time, it would be perfect.

"Finally, Deborah has arranged for the synagogue to provide the wine goblets and carafe of wine for the ceremony, along with the food. You could purchase two goblets to be used in place of the rented ones, and take them with you afterward.

"They could be made of fine crystal, a special wedding present for her and a treasured remembrance of your sacred occasion. Certainly she won't have conceived of such a gift." The rabbie chuckled happily. "She'll be thrilled, and you'll win her love all over again."

I doubt that's possible, Rabbi, but somehow I've got to make it happen.

"I believe your bride-to-be has taken care of everything else."

Ted got to his feet and shook the other man's hand. "I can't thank you enough for your help."

"It's been my pleasure. I have to say I'm looking forward to your wedding."

So am I. Starting tomorrow night, I won't be sleeping alone anymore.

He sensed that tomorrow night would represent the way their marriage was going to go for the rest of their lives. What happened at the ceremony and later, at home, was crucial. And it was his one chance....

Nodding his head goodbye, Ted left the synagogue and drove back to the penthouse. The outcome of his meeting with the rabbi necessitated some shopping. Bernard could help him run down a jeweler who'd be willing to do a rush job. Then they'd have to buy the goblets, and if possible have them some how personalized.

Since the wedding wouldn't take place until sundown tomorrow, there should be time enough to take care of everything—including another surprise having to do with the *ketubah*.

The provision that he would take financial responsibility for Deborah and their child for their entire lives, whether Ted himself was alive or dead, had already been written into the agreement at her uncle's.

But he hadn't forgotten that he owed Deborah's parents a debt of gratitude he could never repay. For their friendship—and for the part they'd played in influencing her to marry him.

Naturally they weren't looking for repayment. It wouldn't occur to them. In fact, their affection for him might turn to dislike if he insulted them by trying to compensate them for what they'd done. Love was their only motive. Love, and having their children's best interests at heart.

However, there was no law that forbade him to add a codicil to the *ketubah* as his way of honoring the Solomon family. Though it could never remove his burden, it would help him remember in the days to come that there'd been at least one act throughout this elaborate scheme to win Deborah back that hadn't been rooted in his own selfishness.

Thinking of her reminded him that she was staying at the Dutchess Inn overnight with her family. When he'd finished all his errands, he had every intention of joining her.

He'd purposely lied to her about the bachelor party so he could talk to the rabbi without her being aware of it. She would assume that he planned to stay out all night enjoying his last hours of bachelorhood.

Nothing could be farther from the truth.

He might not be a Jewish fiancé, but he was a man in love.

The only party he needed or wanted was one with Deborah as the sole guest. In the few short weeks she'd been staying at the penthouse, he'd grown so accustomed to her presence, he couldn't tolerate the idea of not finding her there when he got home.

She thought herself safe from him tonight, hidden

from view behind her relatives. He couldn't wait to see the look on her face when she opened her hotel room door to him. Just the thought made his heart race faster.

"AUNT ELINOR? Why did you tell the taxi driver to take us to the Plaza?"

The family had just finished the celebration dinner. Somehow Deborah had ended up in a taxi with her mother's older sister, who was the most stubborn of the two and spoke her mind more readily than Miriam.

"Because that's where we're going to spend the night. Your uncle Adolph and I planned this special treat just for you."

"But Ted arranged for everyone to stay at the Dutchess Inn. All our things are there!"

"Not anymore."

When it dawned on her what her aunt was up to, Deborah shook her head in exasperation.

"Aunt Elinor—I wish I really *was* the young bride-to-be, hiding from her fiancé, needing to remain pure before her wedding night. But that's not the case. I'm pregnant with Ted's child, and he's at a party with his friends. I love you for trying to make this wedding special, but it just doesn't have the fairy-tale ending you and Mom wanted for me."

"You think I don't know that? You think I don't know how much pain you've been in?"

Deborah's eyes smarted.

"You should have singing and dancing and

laughter at your wedding. You should be joyous. Instead, you walk around like an old woman who knows all her springs have passed her by."

She had no idea her aunt understood so much. "I apologize for being such a disappointment to everyone," Deborah whispered.

"If you mean that, then stop feeling sorry for yourself and behave like a bride."

"I don't know how," she said in a strangled voice.

"That's why I'm here. To help you. You went to him and told him you were pregnant when you didn't have to. He came back for you when he didn't have to. He asked the question and you said 'yes.' You now have a contract. That obligates you to put the past behind you.

"Tomorrow is your wedding, the time when you come clean and sinless to your bridegroom. Tonight is the night of anticipation and excitement."

Deborah bit her lip. "I would give anything if he felt like that—if he was in love with me."

"I believe he is, which is why you need our protection tonight."

The women in her family were hopeless romantics. Deborah had been like that once.

She shook her head in frustration. "This is ridiculous. He's not going to come looking for me. Bernard had plans for an all-night party."

"We'll see. Did I tell you before that I didn't think they could make such a good kosher meal in Poughkeepsie?"

THE DUTCHESS INN was a small luxury hotel Ted always used for important clients, or in this case, Deborah's family. He assumed their celebration dinner was over by now. It was after eleven, but he doubted Deborah would be asleep yet.

"Good evening. I'd like the key to room 214, please."

"Here you are, Mr. Taylor."

He opted for the stairs and took them two at a time to the second floor. At the third door down the hall on his left, he knocked to give warning, then inserted the plastic key card.

The door only opened three inches. She'd put on the chain. Of course he was glad she'd taken precautions against a possible intruder. Right now, though, it frustrated him.

"Deborah?" There was no sound.

"Just a minute."

Suddenly Deborah's father was at the door in his pajamas. He unfastened the chain and opened the door all the way. His hair looked disheveled. He'd been asleep. Hell.

Ted felt like a total idiot. Judging by her father's drawn brows, he considered Ted something much worse than that.

"I'm sorry, Ben. I thought this was Deborah's room."

He made a grunting sound. "Things got switched around. She's not here."

Since Ted couldn't have embarrassed himself any more than he already had, he decided to forego the pretense. Especially in front of Ben, who could see right through him.

"Do you know which room she's in?"

"No, I don't." He turned and called out to Miriam. "Where's Deborah staying tonight?"

"With Elinor!"

"Elinor?"

Ben nodded. "They wanted to do something special for her."

Ted had to clamp down hard on his emotions. His plans for tonight had just gone up in flames.

"If I hear from her, can I give her a message and have her call you in the morning?" He'd made it abundantly clear that his daughter was off-limits.

"The message will keep," Ted muttered. "I apologize for disturbing you and Miriam. Good night."

"Laila Tov."

The door closed in his face.

In less than a minute he approached the receptionist at the front desk and handed over the key. "Which room are the Latermans in?"

"Latermans? Let me see. They checked out earlier this evening."

"Did they leave word where they were going?" Ted demanded.

"No."

"Will you look through your messages?"

"They would be on the computer, Mr. Taylor. There's nothing."

"Will you give me Isaac Solomon's room number?"

"Yes, sir. Room 201."

"Thank you."

He headed for the house phone and dialed the number. It rang a long time.

"Yes?"

Another family member who'd been sound asleep.

"Isaac? It's Ted Taylor. I wouldn't disturb you if this weren't important. Do you know which hotel Adolph and Elinor checked into?"

There was a long pause followed by a deep sigh. "Just a minute while I ask Essie."

Ted counted to ten while he waited.

"She says the Plaza."

"Thank you very much. I'm sorry I had to bother you."

"It's all right. Good night."

Ten minutes later, he was on the Plaza's house phone to the Latermans. He let it ring ten times. No answer. After checking with the front desk to make sure it was the right room, he went over to the phone and tried again.

"Hello, Miriam? Is that you?" At least Elinor sounded awake. He didn't feel quite so guilty.

"No, Elinor. It's Ted."

"Ted! Somehow I didn't expect to hear from you tonight. Are you all right? Deborah said you were at a big party Bernard planned for you."

"It, uh, ended early."

"Are you home then?"

"No. I'm downstairs. Why did you change hotels?"

"Oh...because the Plaza has an indoor swimming pool. It's the perfect way for Deborah to relax before the ceremony."

Deborah didn't like to swim.

"May I speak to her please?"

"She fell asleep about an hour ago. You want me to wake her up?"

"If you don't mind. It's important."

"Is it an emergency? Because if it isn't, she needs her sleep, especially with the baby com—"

"It's an emergency," he blurted. His patience had run out.

"I'll get her. Hold on."

Elinor was gone too long for his liking.

"Ted?"

Deborah's voice. At last.

"What's going on?" he asked without preamble.

"I'm sorry if you've been trying to reach me. I'm afraid you're marrying into a family of people who love tradition. One of those traditions is to keep the bride and groom separated before the ceremony. I told them it was foolish where we're concerned."

I've hurt you so much haven't I, darling?

"How come you're still not at the party?"

"It broke up early."

"Did you enjoy it?"

He grimaced. "Not particularly."

"Aunt Elinor says you're downstairs. Is anything wrong?"

Ted raked a hand through his hair, trying to gather his thoughts.

"No. Yes," he amended. "I didn't like the idea of going back to the penthouse and not finding you there. I'm going to miss you tonight."

"This is the time to enjoy your freedom. It'll end soon enough." Her words hurt.

"After tomorrow night, there's no going back, Deborah. Be very sure this is what you want."

Before the phone clicked off, he heard her say, "I always knew what I wanted."

"DEBORAH? Mind your mother and stand still while I fasten the rest of these buttons."

"So many buttons are going to drive Ted crazy."

"According to Adolph, he's already certifiable."

Deborah heard all four women laugh. Her eyes misted, with tears. *They're loving this. They're all trying so hard to make my wedding day a joyous one.*

"You're a vision in that white silk, sweetheart," her aunt Essie said. "The Empire waist with that high neck is perfect. But your mother's right. If we don't hurry, the ceremony will start without us. Rickie says everyone's already assembled. The rabbi and Ted are waiting."

"It won't hurt to keep the groom worrying a little longer, Essie," Elinor said briskly. "You know, I like this tiara headdress. It makes you look like a queen, Deborah. I think we were right about the lower heels. Now the lace of the dress sweeps the floor the way it should.''

''And those shoes are more comfortable for our mother-to-be.''

''Anna? Go around the other side and be sure her veil hasn't caught on the back part of her head-dress.''

''Wasn't it thrilling last night? Ted looking everywhere for her?''

''It wasn't so thrilling when he couldn't find her, let me tell you. Benjamin said if looks could kill, he'd have been dead before he could undo the chain.''

There was more twittering as the veil was lowered over her face. Her father hadn't told her that part at lunch, about Ted coming to his door, demanding to see her. Deborah felt the heat scorching her cheeks. Thank heaven no one could see.

''That was pure genius to change hotels, Elinor. Ted couldn't speak a civil word to anyone. I didn't think he could get that upset.''

''Wasn't it romantic, the way he was calling around everywhere, not worrying if he disturbed people?''

''I told him Deborah was asleep. He didn't care. He said it was an emergency and ordered me to wake her up.''

The laughter was embarrassing. It was wonderful. Deborah loved her family for being happy about the wedding and treating it like the joyous event she wished it could be. But that only made her guilt worse.

Aunt Elinor spoke the truth last night. I did tell Ted 'yes.' He's expecting me to be a wife in the fullest sense of the word. I don't know if I can.

"She's ready. Thank you, everyone, for helping. Now my daughter and I need a moment alone."

CHAPTER NINE

SUDDENLY THE ROOM had emptied. The noise and gaiety had ceased. Deborah's mother took both her hands.

"A woman's life can be marvelous or it can be terrible," Miriam said quietly. "She can let life happen to her, or she can make life happen. God put the power in her to decide. Make that decision carefully before you leave the canopy, then never complain about it. Now...it's time."

She felt her mother's kiss on her brow through the veil, then they began their walk.

All the people she loved most in the world stood waiting, but the only person she really saw was the man she loved.

It *had* to be love, or she could never have considered his proposal a second time after what he'd done to her.

With each step she absorbed a little more of her mother's wisdom until it seemed to distill throughout her entire being. By the time she'd made her way to Ted's right side, her mind and heart were in accord, and for the first time in months, she experienced a sense of peace. As she'd told him last night, she *did* know what she wanted and always had.

With this acceptance, she felt a surge of relief and cast her eyes in Ted's direction. Bernard, her father and David hovered close by.

Ted, who wore a midnight-blue dress suit, looked beautiful to her.

Her mother held her by the other arm and pulled her away to begin the walk around her bridegroom. Seven circles to signify that he was now the centre of her world. And she of his.

When she came abreast of him for the last time, he was waiting for her. After lifting the veil, he pulled her into his arms. They stood in a semi-embrace before the rabbi, her heart pounding wildly against his chest.

Her gaze darted to the table. Gone were the rental glasses she'd picked out for the wine. In their place were two exquisite crystal goblets that could only have been handcrafted in Venice. Against a background of cobalt blue, an ornate gold *D* was encrusted on one, an ornate gold "*T*" on the other.

How on earth had he thought of anything so beautiful? When had he had them made?

The marriage blessings wafted past her. She drank the wine without tasting it. In a kind of daze, she took the ring from the pillow Rickie handed her and slid it on Ted's finger.

The first ring she'd bought for Ted had long since been returned to a jeweler in Jerusalem. Her mother had helped her pick out this plain gold band when they'd gone shopping in New York. Now it adorned his hand.

Still glassy-eyed, she watched Ted take the ring from the pillow Bernard offered. She automatically put out her left hand, but he only squeezed it. She lifted her gaze, not comprehending.

A ghost of a smile hovered at the corners of his mouth as he reached for her right hand and slid the ring home. When she looked down, she couldn't prevent a swift intake of breath. It wasn't the ring that belonged to the set. It was Ted's.

She'd come across it in his room once when, like every woman in love, she'd wanted to see his child-hood pictures and know every fascinating detail of his life.

It was the only piece of jewelry he'd ever picked up on his travels. Toledo silver, he'd told her. He was a student of Spanish-American history and had done some research in church archives there. He'd confided in her that he hoped someday to write a book on the subject. Another impressive facet of his personality, Deborah had thought, studying the ring.

It was time to read the *ketubah*. The document was larger than she'd anticipated and had been placed on an easel next to the table holding the wine.

Suddenly her veil was lifted, and Ted's blue eyes found hers. Such different eyes from the ones she'd looked into at Graycliff. This time she saw life in them; this time they acknowledged her. But she still detected a lingering shadow.

Pain? Sadness? What put it there?

It didn't used to be there, my darling.

"I love you." He mouthed the words, then stole a kiss from her lips before he lowered the veil, caressing her arm as he did so.

While she pondered these unexpected intimacies, she heard the reading of the financial document. Deborah already knew the amount agreed upon when she'd gone to her uncle's house and only half listened. She was still too bemused by what Ted had done to fully concentrate.

"...And finally, to honor the Solomon family as well as the Holocaust victims who represented a third of the world's Jewish population, an anonymous donation of five million dollars to Yad Vashem, The Martyrs' and Heroes' Remembrance Authority on Har Ha-Zikaron, has been made and noted."

Dear God.

Deborah gasped. She wasn't alone in her shock as other family members echoed their incredulity. Without conscious thought, she grasped his arm to try to tell him what his overwhelming generosity meant to her.

He couldn't know.

He couldn't possibly know what it meant to her. To her parents. To the whole family. To the Jewish people.

She stared now in disbelief, as the Rabbi began the Sheva Brachet, the seven blessings.

There was a tug on her sleeve. Out of the corner of her eye, she saw Rickie extending an object. Jordan and Mary peered over her shoulder with a look of lively anticipation on their faces.

The champagne glass.

Too many wonderful things had been happening. She'd almost forgotten the one part of the ceremony Ted had probably been looking forward to the most.

The glass was usually sheathed in some kind of protective wrapping; in this ceremony it wasn't. That had been Ted's doing.

They drank a second cup of wine, then Deborah leaned down and placed the glass near his shoe. As she straightened, she caught the glint in his eye before he smashed it in one effortless movement of his right foot.

"You're my wife now."

Deborah blushed because the rabbi had been pre-empted by her husband's statement, which was not part of the marriage ceremony. His words reached every corner of the chapel and produced smothered laughter from everyone, including the rabbi.

Mindless of the others, Ted put his arms around her again, drawing her close for the rest of the ceremony.

Deborah tried to focus on the proceedings, but she could feel the force of Ted's gaze, compelling her to look at him. Seconds before the rabbi pronounced the final benediction, she could hold out no longer and gave in to her desire. She turned to him and met his eyes.

Like electricity crackling during a storm, raw energy leapt between them, propelling her closer until their mouths met out of burning need.

As if whipped by the wind, the fire of their kiss exploded, carrying her back to another time when their minds and bodies were extensions of each other, when every thought, every touch was instinctive and familiar.

His hands slid down her back to draw her against him. But neither of them was prepared for the sensation they experienced when the hard mound of her swollen belly suddenly touched him.

Reality asserted itself and brought her back to the present with a jolt as she felt a quickening in her womb and saw the shock reflected in Ted's eyes seconds before he relinquished his hold.

He'd felt the baby move.

With a woman's instinct, she realized the child growing inside her hadn't been real to him before now. Suddenly it had shape and mass. A living entity created out of their passion.

She searched for a sign that this new physical knowledge brought him any joy, any happiness at all. But she couldn't find it. His blue eyes were suddenly shadowed, solemn.

Their baby was the catalyst that had brought them to this.

Their wedding day.

The thought that he might never feel—might never be *able* to feel—genuine love for his son made Deborah vow to cherish this child all the more. And to teach her husband about a parent's love by her own example.

Awareness of her surroundings returned. She felt as if she'd lived a lifetime in his arms although only a minute had passed while their loved ones stood by to watch the bridal couple seal their vows in the time-honored way.

"Shall we greet our guests, Mrs. Taylor?" His question against her lips broke the hushed silence. With a nod from the rabbi, Ted grasped her hand and led her the short distance to the adjoining social hall where everyone converged on them with cries of laughter and delight.

Despite the small size of the gathering, it took long minutes to hug each family member and friend and accept their congratulations before Deborah found herself back in her husband's arms.

"I've missed you" was all he said before he lowered his head and claimed her mouth once more.

Ted was hiding a terrible secret from her. Something so crucial, he'd broken their engagement because of it. Something he couldn't talk about. But he'd always wanted her. In that regard, their relationship hadn't changed except that his desire for her seemed to have grown even stronger.

Having made up her mind to put the past away and embrace her future, she responded to his kiss. It was liberating to answer his passion without holding anything back.

She heard his satisfied groan before he tore his lips from hers and put her at arm's length. His veiled eyes searched hers, as if he didn't quite believe what had just happened.

After everything he'd done to make the ceremony one she'd remember all her life, she wanted— needed—to pour out her heart to him. But David chose that moment to whisper, ''The partying can't begin until you two take the first bites of the *challah.*''

In the nicest possible way, her brother had reminded her that she and Ted were ignoring their guests.

Red-faced, she grasped Ted's hand and led him to a table where the caterers had placed a half-dozen loaves of the special braided bread prepared for sacred occasions.

After Ben had made a blessing over the *challah,* she broke off the end of one and fed it to her husband.

With a wicked grin, he imitated her actions and helped her to an equally healthy bite. Their guests reacted with laughter and applause.

After they'd taken their places at the head table, she felt a hand slide onto her thigh. His touch brought with it a rush of warmth and sent excitement spinning through her body.

It wasn't as if he'd never done anything like this. From the first moment they met, they'd found it impossible to keep from touching each other. But that was before he'd cut her off without any recourse.

Since his return to her life, the pain of that experience had strained every aspect of their relationship. But as her mother had said, she could remain passive, a victim or she could choose to work out her destiny. Deborah had already made her decision by the time she'd reached the marriage canopy.

Obeying a driving need, she covered his hand with her own. Scarcely had she made contact when Ted leaned over and gave her a kiss unlike the others. This was a husband's kiss, frank with longing. She started to tremble.

He seemed to have forgotten where they were. There was still an important part of the celebration to get through, but his response was an unmistakable signal that he wanted to be alone with her.

She heard the scrape of her father's chair and then he was on his feet preparing the champagne glass to be passed among family and friends as they bestowed blessings on the happy couple.

Benjamin cleared his throat with a resounding noise which must have alerted Ted. With obvious reluctance, he let her go. But his hand remained where he'd put it.

Uncle Isaac took the cup without drinking from it and pronounced a blessing of health. Her uncle Adolph followed suit with a blessing of a bounteous and fruitful union. Uncle Marvin invoked a blessing of long life. "To be able to enjoy your grandchildren and your great-grandchildren."

Rickie was the first to stand after Deborah's family had finished. "Ted and I were blessed to have each other," she began. At the sound of his name, Ted's hand tightened on Deborah's leg.

"All the years we were growing up, I dreaded the day when his heart would be captured by a special woman. I knew she'd have to be special because Ted was."

"Rickie..." he murmured under her breath, but Deborah heard him. She knew there had been some estrangement between him and his sister, although she didn't understand the reasons for it. Maybe now, after this, they would resume their former closeness.

"I already didn't like her," Rickie continued, "because she would take away my dearest and best friend, and I didn't know how I was going to stand it."

Rickie's eloquence and sincerity moved Deborah unbearably. Tears started in her eyes. She glanced at her husband; his gaze was fixed on his sister in rapt attention.

"Every girlfriend of mine wanted to be that woman, but to my selfish joy, he seemed to prefer my company to theirs. Until we took a trip to Israel where, quite literally, Deborah Solomon happened to him and he was never the same man again."

Thank you, dear Rickie. Thank you for that.

While Rickie spoke, Deborah's parents were nodding their heads in agreement.

"What made it so easy was the fact that I loved Deborah, too. What isn't there to love? I finally have the sister I always wanted. Thank God that day has come."

"Amen," everyone murmured in a collective voice, amid some sniffling and clearing of throats.

Ted's response was to search for her hand and cling to it.

Bernard got to his feet and took the cup from Rickie. "Before I met Deborah, Ted and Rickie were my two favorite people. When Jordan entered the picture, that number grew to three. Now there's a fourth. Deborah.

"Like Rickie, I didn't think any woman could be worthy of Ted. He'd always been my hero and still is. But then his perfect match came along, when no one would have expected it. I love Deborah, too, and wish you both the joy of your union."

Her heart was so touched, her emotions were growing out of control. When she saw the cup passed to David, she wondered how she could sit through this without embarrassing herself.

Her brother removed his glasses and placed them on the table. "Ted comes from a different life and a different culture than Deborah's," he began. "But he and my sister have proved that love knows no boundaries. Deborah has chosen Ted for her husband.

"Our parents always taught me to take care of my sister and watch over her. It was the easiest thing they ever asked of me. She's a treasure.

"Ted discovered that treasure for himself when he traveled to Jerusalem many months ago. Now it's his right and responsibility to love and protect her. Just remember I'm still here for you, Deborah. I love you."

"I love you," she mouthed to her brother, wiping

her eyes with a napkin Ted handed her. As soon as David was seated, their father stood up. His moist eyes smiled at her and Ted for a long time before he said anything.

"When my beautiful Deborah was born, I had a vision of the kind of man she would marry. My family will understand that vision. I wanted her husband to share her faith and her values, to be kind and strong and compassionate. As she grew into a woman, I began to think maybe this man was good enough for her. Or maybe that one." He gestured with his hands.

"To be honest, I never did see the perfect man for her. There was always something not quite…right. Inside I was glad she did not choose any of them.

"Like Rickie who did not want to give up her brother, I thought selfishly that perhaps Deborah would continue to be happy with her mama and me.

"Just when I started to relax, Deborah came home on leave from the army, took one look at Ted and— it happened!

"'So fast?' I said to myself. 'An American of all people? Not Jewish? So blond and blue-eyed?' Of course, I *could* see how attractive he was, how knowledgeable! He listened to me talk, let me go on about my favorite subjects. Such respect! We exchanged philosophies and he flattered me by telling me how wise I was.

"When our family took him around the museum, I felt his compassion. I watched him share truths with his sister. He urged her to listen so she would understand the magnitude of the Holocaust. What it said about the human race. His capacity to feel that strongly about something so far removed from his own experience told me he was quite exceptional.

"I began to think, how strange! This man feels familiar to me. He speaks to my heart. If it weren't for his outer covering, Ted could be the one I envisioned for my daughter almost twenty-seven years ago. It was the outer covering that had me fooled. Of course, it didn't take Miriam as long to sort out her feelings.

"It didn't take my daughter any time at all. Her heart understood him immediately. I saw the wonder in her eyes. That's when I knew she wouldn't be living with Miriam and me much longer."

He nodded his head. "It was all right. I didn't mind. I'm getting a grandson into the bargain. Not every father can boast of that so soon after the marriage of his favorite daughter."

Deborah stared at her father through wet eyes, overcome by his words. He was a very loving man, but not normally one to express his emotions at length.

"I know I speak for everyone here when I say thank you to my new son-in-law for the donation he has given Yad Vashem. An even greater love than the love he has shown for Deborah and our family has prompted him to do this.

"He has true compassion for mankind and its suffering. I was a witness to that long before he asked me if he could marry my daughter.

"By the world's standards, five million dollars is of the highest significance. In God's eyes, it's the intent of the giver that truly matters. Ted's intent is pure. Therefore it is an acceptable offering and will be used for the common good for years to come.

"Welcome to the family, my son. May you and Deborah continue to grow in your love. May you have peace."

He put the cup in front of them. Deborah drank from it first, then handed it to Ted. As soon as he'd tasted the champagne, the dinner and the conversation could begin.

She glimpsed his eyes for only an instant before he raised the cup to his lips and drank. They were the same eyes she'd seen at Graycliff. Bleak. Hopeless.

Aghast, she turned her head away. She had to get out of the room.

Before he'd lowered the cup, she was on her feet. Touching his arm she leaned over and whispered, "Excuse me for a minute. I should have used the rest room before the toasting started."

"Promise you'll hurry back, darling," Ted called over his shoulder. He knew he should have stood up and escorted her at least as far as the doors, but Ben's heartrending tribute had paralyzed him.

If it weren't for his outer covering, Ted could be the one I envisioned for my daughter.... It was the

*outer covering that had me fooled.... Ted's intent is
pure. Therefore it is an acceptable offering....*

An invisible shudder shook Ted's body. He
wanted to crawl into a dark hole and cover himself.
Hide his shame from these people.

*Benjamin Solomon, if you knew my last name was
von Haase, would the offering still be acceptable?*

*There are pictures of my grandfather at the mu-
seum. Pictures of that monster when he was close
to the age I am now. If you were to compare us, you
would see a chilling resemblance.*

*You haven't noticed because the black-and-white
photographs don't show blond hair and blue eyes....
But I have his same height and bone structure. The
Vampire of Alsace incarnate.*

"Ted? Ted! For the love of God, get a grip on
yourself." Bernard's hushed admonition saved him
from the drowning blackness.

"I can guess what Ben's talk has done to you,
but this is your wedding night. Remember, we'll be
taking care of business soon. If von Haase is there,
we'll find him."

"And if he isn't?" Ted hissed. The violence of
his emotions made the cords stand out in his neck.

"Then we'll search every inch of Paraguay soil
until we have proof one way or another. If he's not
there, we'll go to Argentina next. We'll never stop
until we find him!"

"Oh, God— Why did she get pregnant? Ben
thinks I'm a good man."

"*You are.*"

"Pray our son turns out to have his mother's eyes and hair coloring. Otherwise he could look too much like a von Haase."

"Don't do this to yourself!" Bernard chastised him. "You'll break Deborah's heart a second time if you keep this up."

There was a slight pause. "Quick! Think up a good excuse because Rickie's seen us talking and she's on her way over here to investigate. She mustn't find out what our plans are, so you've got a lot of repair work to do. Rickie's nobody's fool."

"You think I don't know that?"

"Ted?" She'd worked her way around to the back of the head table and come to stand behind his chair. "Is everything all right?"

Thanks to Bernard's intervention, Ted could pull himself together enough to get to his feet. He turned to the sister he cherished and drew her into his arms. It was a relief. He'd been cruel to her. Now was as good a time as any to make amends.

"I love you, Rickie," he murmured as they rocked back and forth. He felt the tension ease out of her. "I love you for all the wonderful things you said tonight. I wanted to say the same things back to you.

"Forgive me for not being there for you the night of your wedding. I have no excuse. I had no right to shut Jordan out. Tell him I'm sorry."

Still in his arms, Rickie started to cry. "I was afraid you hated me for not letting Jordan help you find our...our grandfather. And then I was even more afraid you hated me for inviting Deborah to the wedding. But I had to do it!''

"I realize that now. Deborah's carrying my child. If it hadn't been for you, I would never have known about it. To abandon her in her pregnancy would have been unconscionable.''

"Then you forgive me?''

"There's nothing to forgive.'' He swallowed hard. "Something had to be done, and no one on this earth can get through to me the way you can.''

"You love her, Ted. I know you do.''

"I never denied it. She's my life!''

"You're her life, too.''

"I know,'' he whispered.

"You've given up the search, then?'' The anxiety in her voice told him how much it still mattered to her.

"Yes,'' he lied through his teeth. "The baby has changed everything. You've convinced me to get on with living and forget the past.''

"I'm so thankful!''

I'm sorry for deceiving you, Rickie. You just don't understand.

"What were you and Bernard talking about so intently just now?''

"A little unfinished business to do with the wedding night.''

"Oh—I'm sorry for prying. It's just that when Deborah got up from the table and dashed off like that—''

Rickie didn't miss a thing. He slowly let her go and stepped back.

"She needed to use the rest room. Apparently at this stage of pregnancy..." He let the words drift away. "If she doesn't come back in another minute, I'll go and find her."

"That's all right. I'll do it. I need to freshen up, anyway."

"Thanks." He kissed her cheek. "Tell my new wife I'm missing her desperately. As soon as possible, I'm whisking us out of here."

Rickie's lovely face glowed. "I'll convey the message, brother dear."

She gave Bernard a huge hug and kiss on the cheek, then hurried out of the room.

"Good job," his cousin said softly. "That was close."

"Too close. It's crucial that Rickie never find out what we're doing. Now that I'm married, I wouldn't trust her not to tell Deborah the truth."

"We can't let that happen. There's too much at stake."

"*Amen.*"

THE BATHROOM HAD no chairs or benches. The wall provided the only support and Deborah leaned against it, trying to contain her sobs.

A few hours ago, she'd made up her mind to embrace this marriage fully and completely. But how was she supposed to do that when the man she'd married was in agony? That was the only way to describe what she'd seen.

Her mind raced frantically as she struggled to find a reason for that kind of pain. When she thought of the heartfelt tributes paid to him tonight, particularly by her father who loved Ted like a son and made no secret of it, she was at a loss to understand.

Maybe it was the absence of his parents that was crushing him with grief. They should have been an integral part of the wedding party.

She knew Ted had to do business with his father on occasion. It wasn't as if he had no contact with him at the office.

Was it possible his parents had objected to a mixed marriage? Could they have threatened to disown him if he followed through with it? She supposed that might explain why he'd broken their engagement so abruptly, but somehow she couldn't see it. Ted made his own decisions.

Yet what did she know about the inner workings of the Taylor household? Ted refused to discuss it. Maybe his parents' opinion held more sway with him than she'd realized.

Whatever the reason, they shouldn't have let anything prevent them from seeing their son married. They should have been seated at Ted's other side, celebrating their son's wedding day. Ted's father should have given one of the toasts and shared his feelings of love about his wonderful son with everyone present.

Deborah knew Ted loved her father and had been

deeply touched by his praise. But she also knew that a child needed to hear those special words from his own parents.

The more she thought about it, the more she believed that the tragic rift between the Taylors and their children was responsible for the damage that had blighted Ted's world. If something wasn't done soon, that damage would destroy Deborah and the baby, as well.

You can let life happen to you, or you can make life happen. The choice is yours.

Anger over the pointless pain brought on by their remoteness, by whatever was wrong in that family, put a stop to Deborah's tears. She washed her face and left the bathroom, deciding that the next time Ted had to go out of town on business, she would phone Graycliff and arrange a meeting with his parents to help unravel the mystery.

Her army training had taught her how to confront the enemy without fear. As far as she was concerned, Ted's parents were the enemy. He hadn't wanted her to meet them—but she was his wife now. Her new status gave her the right to come face-to-face with her husband's parents, she decided as she studied the silver ring on her finger.

Rickie had indicated that she hoped it could happen one day. Deborah would ensure that it did.

never forget.

CHAPTER TEN

"DEBORAH?" Ted's sister was coming toward her.
"Ted said you needed to use the rest room, but
when you were gone so long, I started to worry."

"I'm fine," she lied, and threw her arms around
Rickie. "Thank you for saying all those things. I'll
never forget them."

"I meant every word."

"I could have given the same speech about you."

They finally pulled apart and looked at each other.
Rickie's eyes were asking questions. This was one
time Deborah couldn't confide in her.

Meeting Ted's parents for the first time was something she didn't want another soul to know about.
Not until she'd been with them and could make
some kind of assessment.

"Ted was about to go in search of you. I inter-
cepted him and told him I'd find out if anything was
wrong."

"I didn't mean to alarm any of you. I needed to
use the rest room, that's all."

"That's what Ted said. It must be getting uncomfortable."

Deborah nodded. "And inconvenient, like right in
the middle of my own wedding feast!"

She smiled. "This was a magnificent wedding, Deborah. Every gesture meant something significant. I loved it."

"I did, too." Her voice trembled. "I'm just so sorry I had to leave yours. When Ted wouldn't acknowledge my presence at the reception, David rushed me away because he knew I was ready to collapse."

"I know. I saw what happened. That was a painful moment for all of us."

"It was horrible. And I never got to tell you how lovely you looked in your wedding dress. You and Jordan made a breathtaking couple.

"I saved some magazines that covered the wedding. The pictures are wonderful! Some day our son will love looking at his aunt and uncle on their wedding day."

"Thank you, Deborah." They hugged again. "Jordan and I would have preferred a quiet little wedding in Father DeSilva's tiny chapel in the Chaco, and Stoney as the only witness." She paused. "You know that Father DeSilva is the reason we've been able to rescue the Indian families? Jordan and I think the world of him.

"But I wanted to bring my parents a little happiness, so we had the wedding at Graycliff and went all out for their sakes. Mother worked on the preparations with me."

"Did they appreciate it?"

"I think so. They can't open up and express themselves. When I'm with your family, the difference is like night and day.''

Deborah shook her head in frustration. ''What's wrong with your parents, Rickie? What made them like that? You and Ted are entirely different!''

A shadow crossed her friend's face. For a moment, Deborah was reminded of Ted in his agony. Additional proof that the Taylors' problems lay at the root of their children's sorrow.

''Something in their early childhoods, no doubt.''

''Something horrible, you mean. Bernard told me his parents were the same way. Now that his mother's gone, he says his father never talks anymore.''

''That's true.'' She smoothed the hair off her forehead. ''His parents' behavior has put Bernard off marriage. He dates casually, but he won't make a commitment. His private secretary, Jill, has been in love with him for several years. But he pretends he isn't aware of her feelings. It's a crime.

''Oh,'' she cried softly, ''let's not talk about it anymore. You're about to enjoy your wedding night. Come on. Ted's waiting.''

They started walking toward the hall, where Deborah could hear laughter and all the familiar sounds of her family and friends enjoying their food and each other.

In a confiding tone Rickie whispered, ''I might as well tell you now that Ted and Bernard were plotting the minute you left the table.''

''They do that a lot. Especially lately.''

Rickie's eyes sparkled. "I couldn't get it out of my brother where he's taking you on your honeymoon, but judging by their secrecy, it's going to be wonderful."

"Then they were putting on an act for your sake, Rickie. We're going back to the penthouse tonight."

Her expression darkened. "What do you mean?"

"After Tahiti, I can understand why you think that sounds boring. But honestly, I'm happy about it. "One day when you're as pregnant as I am, you'll understand why I'd rather stay put. Ted and I talked it over and decided we'll have a honeymoon after the baby is born. Besides, we're both excited about moving into our house."

Rickie stared at her as if she'd never seen her before. Deborah couldn't understand her odd reaction; it was almost as though Rickie didn't believe her. "When does that take place?" her sister-in-law asked.

"Day after tomorrow."

"Why so soon? Couldn't it have waited a couple weeks, just to give you time to rest after all the wedding plans?"

"No. Ted has a big banking conference in Switzerland coming up around that time."

"Switzerland? For that he can send one of the vice presidents. It's quite routine."

"He and Bernard have other places they're going too. Anyway, it'll take a while to settle into the house. By the time he leaves, I'll be able to spend time with you and Mary. I'd like to help out with those Indian families if you'll let me."

"I'd love that," Rickie murmured, but Deborah thought she sounded far away. "I'm just sorry to hea—"

"I know what you're going to say," she interrupted. "None of this sounds very romantic to you. That's why Ted pretended otherwise. But I prefer it this way. "Rickie…every minute I ever spent with him was like one glorious honeymoon. We took small trips to Greece when I could get the time off. There were nights—"

"I know," Rickie broke in, sounding equally affected. "It was like that with Jordan in the Chaco, in Tahiti. It's that way now. I want it to be that way again for you and Ted."

So do I.

And I refuse to let my husband's pain prevent us from achieving that kind of joy.

THE BLUE BATHROBE she'd bought for him in Crete hung on the back of his bathroom door. Earlier in the day she'd hidden his wedding present in one of the pockets, thinking he'd find her gift the next time he showered. But her plans had changed.

On the way home, as Bernard drove the newly-weds from the synagogue to the condo, she'd figured out what she had to do if she wanted this marriage to take hold. And she did. The possibility of its not working had been stricken from her thoughts.

She was no longer the same woman who'd left

the penthouse at four-thirty in the afternoon as Deborah Solomon. That Deborah had been living in the guest bedroom.

She had expected to return to that room after the wedding because she wasn't sure she was over the pain of Ted's rejection enough to make love to him again.

He'd been incredibly patient. She knew that if she felt the same reluctance tonight, even though it was their wedding night, he would still make no demands.

But the sage advice her mother had given her before their walk to the marriage canopy, plus the pain she'd seen in Ted's eyes at the wedding dinner, had created a profound change in her.

Like a person fitted with the right pair of lenses, she saw her path clearly, where before it had been indistinct.

After a quick shower, she slipped into his robe and tied the belt loosely around her protruding stomach. She used a couple of towels to dry her freshly shampooed hair, then braided it so it hung down her back.

He was somewhere in the penthouse, turning off lights, seeing to whatever needed doing. When he came to bed, he would find he was not alone.

As she entered his room, the soft glow from a bedside lamp revealed her husband stretched out on the king-size bed. He lay on his side in a relaxed position, facing her, his head propped in his left hand.

The comforter covered the lower half of his body. His bare chest and arms had been left exposed.

He remained very still and didn't smile. There wasn't a nervous muscle in his body. His half-veiled gaze traveled up her legs, over her pregnant curves covered by the robe and rested on her hair.

"You're being so brave, Deborah. You don't have to."

"You mean you don't want me?"

His face darkened. "I love you in all the ways a man can love a woman. But I hurt you." He sighed. "My one fear about the donation I made today was that you might feel I...bought you. And that you might consider it your duty to sleep with me again."

"Duty has nothing to do with it. She strolled toward him. "If I didn't know better..." She brushed her lips against his as she knelt on the bed next to him. "I would say you were afraid to touch me. Is it because I'm pregnant? Don't worry. Our son is deep inside me, warm and safe. He'll never know what's happening," she teased with a seductive smile.

He traced a finger along the outline of her mouth. "You're so beautiful." A film of moisture intensified the blue of his eyes, no longer clouded by shadow. "I don't deserve you."

"If you don't, then who?" She smiled to cover her puzzlement. *Deserve* was a word he'd never used in their relationship before.

Why don't you deserve me?

"Tonight when your father talked about the man

his Deborah would marry one day, I could picture him clearly.''

"So could I. That afternoon in Jerusalem. The minute I saw you sitting on the couch next to my father.'' She smiled at the memory. "The two of you were in the middle of a discussion. It struck me how much you were enjoying each other. My father's eyes always mirror his thoughts. When he's being polite, they remain impassive. They were shining the whole time they rested on you.

"Mother sat in the chair on your left. She didn't perch on the edge, as if she had to be ready to play hostess. She was sitting back, listening.

"I remember that she wore the loveliest smile. It's a look of contentment, the look she gets when everything's right. It was the look on her face at the ceremony tonight. Very simply, it said you belonged there. They knew it. I knew it.''

"Deborah…''

He drew her close to him, settling her against the pillows so he could look down at her. They studied each other quietly.

His thoughts went back to that moment months ago when she'd come rushing into her parents' living room dressed in her army fatigues, carrying a rifle. Lord, she was something.

"Do you remember the first time we made love? It was by the sea and we'd stayed up all night talking. The smell of the desert air had intoxicated us. We'd eaten cherries we bought at a stand. Your mouth was stained a deep red. Do you remember how hot the sun was, even though it was still so early?

"The warmth felt so good." She smiled.

"The light gilded your skin. It showed me those velvety brown eyes, your beautiful long lashes. I'd never seen your beauty so clearly.

"I remember unraveling your braid. Its glossy brown texture delighted me. I wanted to see the individual strands in the light. So many beautiful colors swirled around my fingers. I hope you won't be offended or find this silly, but—it reminded me of Erma's chocolate marble cake."

"Wasn't she one of the cooks at Graycliff?"

"That's right. Our favorite person. She always had time for Rickie and me. When we were little, we used to watch her make it. That's one of my few happy memories of my childhood—being in the kitchen with Erma. She would drop the chocolate batter into the white batter, then draw a knife through it. We were fascinated by the range of colors, from the lightest brown to a rich dark chocolate.

"You looked delicious like that. I remember how much I wanted to taste you. I thought if I could take all of you into myself, consume you, I would never be cold again because you would be alive inside me. A warm, living, vital part of me."

"Ted—"

"My instincts were right. Tonight there's no sea, no sand, no sun. The air isn't the same. But none of that matters. The warmth radiates from within you. The color of your mouth needs no cherries for enhancement. No perfume from a desert wind could smell as divine as your skin and hair.

"I want to love you all night, my Deborah. Close your eyes."

Afraid to breathe, she obeyed him, wanting the moment to go on forever. She didn't know this Ted who was sharing so much more than he'd ever shared before.

The man whose sorrow could turn him into someone else wasn't in evidence now. How she wished that man would be gone forever....

"Oh—" She let out a surprised cry. He'd fastened a piece of jewelry around her neck. A pendant of some kind. Was it a medal? She felt its cool weight against her skin.

"You can look now."

She opened her eyes.

He lifted it for her inspection. Another cry escaped her lips.

From the silver chain hung a Star of David fashioned in silver, about one and a half inches in size. The center was cut out. Six triangular diamonds filled in the triangles. Their sparkling brilliance reminded her of a cluster of stars pulsating in a Judean sky.

"I—It's too beautiful." Her voice caught. "I've never seen one like this."

"I had it specially made for you months ago in Jerusalem. The artisan had wanted to fashion it in gold, but I insisted on silver. I knew how perfect it would look against your skin, your hair. Now I'm doubly glad. It goes with your ring.

"I'm hoping that when you wear this particular star, you'll see us in it. Naturally the top triangle represents your striving toward God. But when you look at the bottom triangle, the one striving toward the real world, you'll think of me."

Deborah burst into tears and buried her face against his shoulder. "You do too much," she half sobbed. "You've given me too much. It's humbling in a way I can't quite describe."

She clutched his arms. "You must have spent hours with the rabbi to come up with so many surprises during the ceremony."

"I did it for my own survival," he said with exaggerated seriousness. "Can you imagine how I would've felt to find someone else under that veil?"

His comment made her laugh despite her tears. She lifted her head to look at him. "I have a surprise for you, too. It's nothing like this pendant," she murmured, kissing it. "But it has special significance for me."

Without preamble she reached in the robe pocket for his gift. "Here."

"What is it?"

"Take a look first." Her excitement was contagious.

"All right." He lifted the lid of the small box and pulled a round gold pocket watch from the tissue. It was a little larger than an American silver dollar, with a fine gold-mesh chain. The numbers on the face had been fashioned in Roman numerals.

"It belonged to my grandfather, my mother's father. Turn it over."

Intrigued, he did and saw the outline of a boat that had been etched in the gold. "It's a replica of the boat on the monument you saw at Yad Vashem, the boat that carried the Danish Jews to Sweden during the Holocaust.

"My grandfather's family had emigrated to Denmark from Poland years earlier. When the Nazis were rounding up Jews, he and his brother got their families to safety on that boat before the two of them, along with several hundred others, were captured and taken to van Haase's death camp in Alsace."

He nodded. "I remember your mother telling me about it."

"Well, this watch was a prized possession, he gave it to my grandmother the night they had to part. Years later, after both families emigrated to Israel, she gave it to my mother.

"Before I went into the army, mother had the engraving done and gave it to me as a reminder to always remember the past, but to be thankful for the future.

"The first time you asked me to marry you, I knew I wanted to give you this watch as a wedding present because I was so thankful to have met you. That feeling has only grown stronger. I want you to keep it as a token of my love. Perhaps one day, when you think the time is appropriate, you can give it to our son."

All the while she'd been talking, he hadn't said anything. His eyes were shuttered, making it difficult to read their expression. She didn't know if she had pleased him or not. After everything had been so perfect, she couldn't bear for there to be any shadows tonight. Not now...

Finally she heard him expel a breath. "I love you for wanting to give me something so precious, but I can't accept it," he said in a thick voice. "I'm not worthy of such a gift, Deborah. I don't deserve it."

That word again.

Ted had gone away from her to a place she couldn't follow. The watch had triggered something negative, some feeling or memory she couldn't understand. She *wanted* to understand. Her desire to talk to his parents had grown into a full-blown need.

Quietly she put the watch back in the box. In the morning she would hide it. For tonight it could stay under the bed.

With that accomplished, she switched off the lamp and moved toward him. The darkness was good. She'd rather not see his demons working to destroy what was left of their wedding night.

"I love you," she murmured against the back of his neck. She put her arms around him, cocooning his hard-muscled body as best she could.

"In this position, our little boy is making it difficult to get as close to you as I'd like. If you'd turn around, I think we can figure out something that will be infinitely more satisfying.''

There was no response. She didn't mind. It was enough to be his wife, to have the right to share his bed and bear his child. She knew he loved her. With enough love she would eventually reach him, eventually get through to him, until he couldn't deny her any part of his soul.

Exhausted by the events of this sacred day, she kissed her pendant before sinking into a dreamless sleep, still embracing her husband.

HE LISTENED to her breathing and knew the exact moment she'd fallen asleep. Carefully he extricated himself from her arms and slid off his side of the bed. After pulling on a pair of boxers he grabbed from his dresser, he headed for the study, and the telephone.

"Bernard?"

"I don't believe it! Good Lord, Ted. It's three in the morning.''

"Tell me about it.''

"What's wrong? Is Deb—"

"The problem is me,'' he cut in harshly.

"I don't understand. When I dropped you two off—"

"She hadn't given me her wedding present yet. Of all the gifts she might have chosen…'' His voice broke.

"What did she do that's turned you inside out like this?''

"Listen." For the next few minutes Ted told him about her gift and the history behind it. There was a stunned silence coming from the other end. "Maybe now you have some inkling of what this night has been like for me."

"Ted? Whatever it takes, we'll find von Haase."

"If he's still alive."

"Forget him for tonight. Don't make her suffer any more than she already has. You only get one wedding night. Make it count."

Bernard's words pierced his defenses.

What kind of monster am I?

How could I have treated her gift like that when it meant so much to her?

How could I have turned my back on my wife on our wedding night?

"I've got to hang up now."

"Ted? I know how much you love her. Good luck."

DEBORAH HAD ALWAYS been a quiet, sound sleeper. He entered the bedroom, satisfied that she hadn't noticed his absence.

Removing his boxers, he slid under the covers and approached her. During her sleep the robe had fallen open. He didn't have to bother with the tie to begin kissing her.

The fear that she might not be able to respond after what he'd done to her tonight almost prevented him from reaching out to her. But he'd underestimated his bride, whose unqualified love didn't ask questions or require explanations.

Instead he heard those familiar little moaning sounds as she strained toward him, seeking his mouth. After being lost in the freezing outer darkness, he was once again welcomed to her fire. The inevitable conflagration consumed them both.

It was like they'd never been apart.

TED PULLED DEBORAH'S CAR to a stop in the parking lot behind the hangar where his father kept a private fleet of jets at the Poughkeepsie Airport.

This would be their first separation since the wedding. They'd spent all night saying goodbye. Neither of them was ready to let the other go.

He'd told Deborah he didn't want her to stand around waiting to see him off. One final kiss in the car was all he could handle, then he wanted her gone.

The sight of those beautiful brown eyes swimming in tears had the power to make him do just about anything—except put off this crucial trip.

"I'm going to miss you so horribly. Promise me you'll call me as often as you can?"

"I swear it, Deborah."

He pulled her into his arms one last time. Though he expected to return, there was a definite risk that neither he nor Bernard would make it back.

If, God forbid, he should be killed, he'd done everything possible to make certain she would never want for anything. He also had the reassurance that she'd always be surrounded by family and friends who would love her and take care of her and their baby.

"I don't see Bernard." She wiped her eyes. They glinted like the diamonds in the pendant she wore day and night.

My cousin has had to make a lot of preparations behind your back, my love.

"He had some last-minute business to attend to at the office, but he'll be here soon. I have to go. If you can't reach me on the cell phone for some reason or other, don't worry. I'll be phoning you as often as I can."

He forced himself from the car to help her change places. Once she was behind the wheel, he pulled his suitcase from the back seat. This one served as camouflage so Deborah wouldn't become suspicious. The other luggage with the kinds of clothes he'd need for their trip to Chaco had been put on board yesterday.

He leaned inside the open window to give her one hard, final kiss.

"You'd better go, darling. Otherwise you might be late for your doctor's appointment. Let me know how you like your new obstetrician."

"I will. Come back soon. I love you." Her voice quavered on the last words.

"You're my life, Deborah. Remember that." He kissed two fingers, then touched them to her lips. She nodded bravely, then drove off. He watched until her car disappeared around the corner.

I'm doing this because I have to. Otherwise I couldn't go on living this lie now that I'm married to you.

He strode swiftly toward the jet parked outside the hangar, anxious to set his and Bernard's intricately laid plans into motion.

"Hi, Mack. How's it going?" he called to the chief mechanic who was busy doing the preflight check. He'd once been a pilot for Ted's father.

"Not bad at all. How's the new bridegroom?"

"Terrific."

"With a lovely lady like that, you ought to be. How come she's not going to Switzerland with you?"

Only the pilot knew their flight plan.

"She's pregnant and the doctor doesn't want her to fly anymore."

"I didn't know that. Congratulations."

"Thank you. When Bernard arrives, tell him I've already gone on board."

"Will do. Have a good trip."

"Thanks, Mack. Take care of yourself."

He hurried around to the door on the side of the private jet and let himself inside.

"Hello, Ted."

He froze in place at the rear of the plane. Rickie?

"Before you try to pretend that you're happy to see me, I'll put you out of your misery by telling you straight out that I know you never had any intention of going to Switzerland."

Damn.

"Where else would I be going?" He stashed his suitcase and walked slowly up the aisle toward her.

"The Chaco."

"That's funny. Mack just asked me why I wasn't taking Deborah to Switzerland with me."

"Don't you remember Mack's always had a soft spot for me and tells me things I want to know? When I started asking questions, he said you had some other luggage put onboard yesterday afternoon."

The onset of anger sent the adrenaline spurting through his veins. "You've been spying on me!"

"No. I simply put two and two together the night of the wedding. Deborah told me there'd be no honeymoon, no trip to Geneva with you. It all became clear, especially your agreement to stop hunting for our grandfather. You capitulated too easily."

She took a deep breath; he said nothing. What *could* he say?

"Dammit, Ted, how could you do this to Deborah now?" Her pain-filled cry rang through the plane's interior.

"This is none of your business, Rickie. I've left Jordan and Stoney out of it, as I promised."

"You lied to me!"

She wasn't about to back down. Hell, she didn't even flinch. They'd come to a total impasse.

"Don't lose any more sleep over it. Go back to your husband and forget me."

"You'll be killed, Ted! I don't know what schemes you and Bernard have hatched, but I can tell you that without someone like Jordan to help you, you haven't got a chance of surviving. Father DeSilva was very emphatic about that."

He cocked an eyebrow. "Your faith in me is very flattering. But Bernard and I aren't businessmen for nothing."

"Business— Those men down there are *evil*. Murdering people is their only business. You have a wife and child to think of now. You have—"

"We have a date with destiny." Bernard insinuated himself between them.

Ted turned his head. His cousin had boarded the plane without making a sound. Thank God he'd come when he had.

"That was very eloquent, Bernard," Rickie lashed out. Her cheeks were splotched a feverish red. "But let's call this what it really is. A date with death, and you both know it!"

Bernard remained unmoved. "We're doing what we have to do, Rickie."

"You can say that so easily, can't you, Bernard? You don't have a wife, let alone a child. You've conveniently avoided those entanglements—so you can support Ted in this insane desire to find von Haase."

"You didn't think it was insane before you met Jordan."

"Because he showed me a better way!" she almost shouted.

"That's fine. That's good. We're happy for you.

But Ted and I have been shown another way. We won't stop until we've accomplished our purpose."

"Until you're dead, you mean."

"It's possible," Ted interjected. "It's thanks to you that I married Deborah. If anything happens to me, she now has my name and financial backing to keep her and the baby for the rest of their lives.

"Knowing Jordan loves you and will always be there for you leaves me free to do what I have to do without regrets."

Rickie started to speak but Ted interrupted her. "Think if we're successful in finding our grandfather and we can force him to stand trial. It will help close a door on the pain of millions of people."

"Will it close a door on your *pain?*" she blurted, before she pushed past both of them.

She paused at the exit. Her face was contorted by anguish. "Will your deaths bring comfort to Deborah and the son you might never see? To your in-laws? To all the people who love you? To our parents? To me?

"I used to think what our parents did to the three of us was the worst way anyone could hurt me. But I was wrong."

CHAPTER ELEVEN

GRAYCLIFF LOOKED different in the chilly morning air without several thousand people milling about its grounds. Except for a few men working in the gardens, the colossal monument appeared empty in its mid-November setting. Lonely.

How strange that Ted and Rickie had grown up here, isolated from other people. Deborah felt an ache for two children who had lived such abnormal lives inside its stately walls. They were blessed to have had each other.

She got out of her car and started walking up the drive toward the front staircases, built—ironically enough—in the shape of a heart. Graycliff supposedly resembled a famous château of the Loire Valley in France. Something out of a fairy tale like *Sleeping Beauty*.

After pondering long and hard, she'd decided to drop in without giving his parents notice. Ted had once mentioned that they traveled a good deal of the year. They might not be here.

She didn't care. Now was as good a time as any to call on his mother and father.

Besides, she was in no particular hurry to go home when Ted wouldn't be there for the next few days. Saying goodbye to her husband an hour ago had been one of the hardest things she'd ever had to do. He'd taken her heart with him.

Since their wedding night, there'd been no more episodes of incapacitating grief. Happily he'd turned to her before morning and made up for it. The rapture of their reunion and the days and nights of love-making that followed had brought her contentment. More than contentment—indescribable joy.

The added excitement of transforming their new house into a home had filled her with energy and purpose. Which was a good thing, since without Ted there, she needed to stay busy.

She looked up the broad expanse of stairway. Now that she was over seven and half months pregnant, the climb was a little daunting. Still, by the time she reached the top she hadn't fared too badly, thanks to the army's rigorous physical training program.

She planned to get back on a good exercise program after the baby was born. Ted had promised to take her on a honeymoon after her six-week checkup. She intended look beautiful for him in every way.

A middle-aged woman who appeared to be the housekeeper answered the door. She stared at Deborah with incurious eyes until Deborah introduced herself. Then she seemed taken aback.

"Ted's wife? Were they expecting you?"

"No. I thought I'd drop in for a visit. Are they home?"

"Yes. You're fortunate to catch them. They're leaving for the Orient in the morning."

Deborah couldn't believe her luck. "Wonderful. Would you tell them I'm here?"

"You can tell them yourself if you like. They're in the rose garden. When they're not abroad, they spend every morning outside, weather permitting."

"Is that the garden beyond the right wing, where Rickie's wedding reception took place?"

"Yes."

"Then I know where it is and I'll find them. Thank you."

"You're welcome."

Deborah felt the woman's eyes on her as she descended the stairs. She could tell the housekeeper didn't know what to think, but at least Deborah hadn't been prevented from seeing them.

She had only a vague idea of what they looked like from the publicity photos of Rickie's wedding reception. She'd garnered an impression of patrician features, trim figures, elegant clothes, nothing more. In the candid shots they were surrounded by other people.

Neither Ted nor Rickie had ever shown her a picture of them, posed or otherwise. She hadn't seen them at the reception. They'd been standing on the other side of Rickie and Jordan, outside of Deborah's line of vision.

Rickie suspected that this vastly wealthy couple, who for the whole of their lives had ignored their children's emotional needs, were among the most egocentric human beings she would ever meet. She imagined they possessed a large dose of prideful arrogance, probably combined with an intimidating hauteur.

Judging by everything she'd heard and surmised, these were cold, unfeeling people.

Deborah had wanted to like them. She had already gone so far as to forgive them in her heart. Something in their lives that had cut them off from ordinary human emotion, and to her that meant they were more to be pitied than censured.

A child wasn't born without feelings. That behavior had to be learned. What horrible experience had they undergone to burn it all away?

Unfortunately their infamous reputation had preceded them, doing its damage. Right now Deborah had few, if any, expectations. Most likely nothing would be accomplished by this visit, but for the sake of her marriage she had to try to get some answers.

Then she saw them, a mid-sixtyish couple in smart yet casual clothes, walking through the garden whose rose bushes had been neatly pruned for winter. The two of them appeared normal in every way.

Both were fair, although as Deborah drew closer she noticed that Ted's mother, of medium height, was going gray. At one time his father had probably had hair like his son's, but it had thinned out and gleamed a dark silver in the morning light. He looked shorter than Ted with a slighter build.

"Hello?" she called from a distance because they

hadn't noticed her yet and she didn't want to startle them.

They both turned in her direction and watched in silence as she approached them. When she got within five feet of them, she came to a standstill. A chill threaded through her body.

Ted's eyes had held the sorrow of the world. Their eyes were dead. They looked a hundred years old.

She felt as if she might throw up, but there was no place to be sick. She wanted to run, but her body stayed frozen in place.

You came for answers.

"My name is Deborah Solomon Taylor. I'm Ted's wife. I'm sure Rickie has told you about me, even if Ted hasn't. As you can see, I'm expecting his child.

"We're going to have a boy at the end of December. I love your son very much, and thought it was time we met."

Neither of them moved, but she detected an inner flinching. Not out of any sense of superiority over her or revulsion because of her. Quite the contrary.

They reminded her of victims of war. Shell-shocked people so horrified by what they'd seen, they couldn't endure even ordinary life anymore.

"How do you do?" His mother spoke first. His father only nodded.

They've lost the capacity to feel. It's what you expected. You have part of your answer, Deborah.

"Come over here, please."

Deborah followed them to a charming area of the garden where two marble benches had been placed in a semicircle. Viewers could enjoy the geometric design of the sculptured hedges and rose trees.

She saw Mrs. Taylor grasping her husband's hand, as if to give him support before they sat down. He wasn't an old man. He didn't need physical help. It was the kind of gesture Deborah had occasionally seen her mother give her father when he needed buoying up.

Mr. Taylor seemed to be the more emotionally crippled of the two.

My husband's role model.

"Are you and Ted happy?"

To Deborah's stunned surprise, she heard a note of urgency in his mother's voice. It was the kind of question Deborah's own mother might ask. It said that she cared, that she worried. His father merely looked on. His pale eyes were a watery blue. Tears?

The two of them were a complete enigma to Deborah. She didn't know what to think. She had to throw out all her preconceived notions and start over.

"We would be completely happy if I knew how to take Ted's sadness away," she said frankly. "He's struggling with something he can't talk about. You must know what it is. Ted has never said the words. Can you help me understand?"

His mother's gray eyes fell.

"He…perceives that we failed him." Mr. Taylor spoke at last.

"But why does he feel that way?" Deborah cried.

"You love our son very much," his mother said. Deborah could tell she didn't want to answer the question. "Otherwise you wouldn't have come to see us when he's forbidden it—Rickie told us that. We're thankful, aren't we?"

Mr. Taylor nodded. "With your love, he will be the father to his son that he wished I could have been to him. Don't tell him you've come to see us."

Deborah could hardly breathe. "But that's so wrong! You obviously love him."

His mother was gazing off into the distance. "We love both our children more than you could ever know. We gave them the only life we knew how to give. Let that be enough."

Again Deborah could hear the pleading.

They had a secret. They didn't want to talk about it. They were in pain and had been running away from it all their lives. How utterly tragic.

The longer Deborah stayed, the more pain she would inflict on them. She could feel it. They wanted this conversation to end.

"You want me to leave, don't you?"

They both looked so uncomfortable, she felt wretched for having asked the question. "I'm sorry for you disturbing you. I'll go. Thank you for talking to me." As Deborah turned to leave, his mother got up.

"Our son is a lucky man."

"Thank you," Deborah whispered before she

hurried away, her thoughts racing ahead to her husband.

Rickie might or might not know their secret, but Ted knew. If he didn't unburden himself soon, he could end up like them. *I can't let that happen, but what can I do about it?*

"I DON'T KNOW about you, but I think I'm quite handsome this way."

Bernard had strolled in from the bathroom to come and stand next to Ted before the hotel-room mirror.

The two Hispanic-looking men staring back from the glass had gained two inches in height. The false bottoms of their specially made boots carried knives. They could only hope that when they were searched by Oriana's men, the boots would escape detection.

With dark wigs, dark contact lenses and makeup, they'd created a transformation so complete, Ted had difficulty believing it was really them.

The disguise was not meant to fool Oriana. Rather, it would help protect Dr. Arbizu, Oriana's go-between, in case he was being watched by those within the country who knew of his association with the general. Two blond Americans in his company would send up a red flag. Not only that, neither Ted or Bernard wanted to draw undue attention to themselves.

"We'd be right at home in Spain. Two fine Castilian medical students in doctor's whites."

"Arbizu won't recognize us when we show up at the hospital."

"Then we'll know we've done this right. How much time before we have to be over there?"

"Enough for you to give Deborah a call. I'm going downstairs to buy us some cigarettes. I swear every man I see carries a pack in his front shirt pocket."

"Good idea. I'll meet you in the foyer in ten minutes."

Ted reached for the room phone and dialed his home number. She'd probably tried to reach him, but this was the first chance he'd had to call her. He yearned to hear her voice.

It was seven in the evening, Asunción time, which meant six o'clock in New York. She should long since have returned home from the doctor's office. There were still boxes of books to unpack. He knew of several projects she'd mentioned that would keep her busy while he was away.

"Hello?"

"Deborah?"

"Ted! I've called you a dozen times."

He let out the breath he'd been holding. "I'm sorry. I've been doing business all day and couldn't really talk until now. How did the appointment go?"

"Fine. Dr. Lambert is very nice, very thorough. He said everything's looking good for a normal delivery."

"That's excellent. What have you been doing all day?"

There was the slightest hesitation before she said, "Just working around the house."

He frowned. Something was wrong. She sounded distracted. He could feel it. "What are you doing right now?"

"Actually I'm just getting ready to go over to Stoney's to help Rickie with the Indian children. She and Jordan have moved into their new house, and they've told me I can stay in their vacant apartment at the hangar."

He recalled the scene on the plane, and a fine film of perspiration broke out on his brow. What was his sister up to?

In his heart of hearts, he didn't believe she would betray him to Deborah. On the other hand, he had to admit he'd never seen her as angry and upset as she'd been this morning.

"When was this decided?"

"At the wedding I mentioned that you'd be going to a conference in Switzerland. A few days ago she called me about it because she knew I'd be lonely without you."

That explanation sounded more like it.

"I miss you so much!" she cried.

His eyes closed tightly. "Not as much as I miss you. Enjoy yourself over there."

"I will. Where are you right now?"

"Getting ready to go to a boring dinner. I'll probably be out too late to phone you tonight, but I'll call tomorrow. Bernard's signaling me to hurry."

"I guess I have to let you go. I wish you were here."

"Me, too. I keep remembering last night." Lord. Last night...

"I wish it'd never ended."

"So do I. Take care, my love."

"Good night."

He inhaled deeply before replacing the receiver. Then he reached for the doctor's bag holding fifty thousand dollars' worth of guaraníes and left the room to join Bernard.

Again he did a double take when he spotted his cousin in the front foyer looking at a brochure he'd taken from the counter. Rickie knew him better than anyone, but even she would gasp in disbelief if she were told the Hispanic stranger in white was her cousin.

Bernard put the brochure back when he saw Ted coming. "Everything okay with Deborah?"

"She's fine."

"That's good. Shall we go?"

A short time later, the taxi dropped them off at the entrance to Government Hospital. Arbizu had said to meet him by the cashier's window of the outpatient clinic.

Bernard's eyes smiled at Ted in amusement as they stood where they were supposed to be while the doctor paced back and forth near the window, his frown deepening as he periodically checked his watch, wondering why they hadn't shown up yet.

Ted decided to put him out of his misery. "*Señor?* We're ready when you are."

Dr. Arbizu's shocked expression was classic. "I had no idea it was you. Your disguises are even better than I had imagined." The older man's nervous smile disappeared. "Follow me. We'll be taking an ambulance van to the compound. Everyone will assume you are my assistants."

"That was the idea. After you, Doctor."

Darkness had settled over the Chaco. The three of them sat in the front seat. They'd left the main highway with its tall poinsettias an hour earlier and were now being jostled as they bumped along the lonely dirt road bordered by scrub palms and savanna.

The nearer they came to Stroessnerplatz, the more wooded the terrain appeared. Ted recognized the quebracho trees but wondered about some of the others. When the doctor refused to answer questions, even about the flora and fauna, he realized the man had his orders to keep quiet.

Finally the headlights exposed a sentry gate ahead, partially hidden by dense foliage. The van slowed down as four armed guards stepped in front of it. Ted didn't doubt that other guards not visible had machine guns pointed at them.

Dr. Arbizu rolled down the window and spoke to them in Spanish. They fired a volley of Spanish words in return.

"We are expected," Arbizu told them, "but you

have to get out and be searched before we can proceed.''

"Understood,'' Bernard muttered as they exited the van.

The fact that the two of them had already made a big donation to the general's war chest probably accounted for the indifferent way the search was carried out. Neither Ted nor Bernard was manhandled. No one stripped them or confiscated their clothes—or boots.

The inevitable blindfolds were tied on, and then they were handcuffed and helped back inside the van. Ted knew that he and his cousin were at the mercy of Dr. Arbizu. Instead of driving them through the gate, he'd turned around and headed in another direction. They'd gone probably two more miles before the van slowed to negotiate two right turns, then a left. Soon they came to a stop.

There were sounds of more voices and footsteps. Once out of the van, Ted felt his arms taken by the guards, then found himself being propelled up some steps into a building. They walked him through several rooms.

Someone freed his hands and removed his blindfold.

"Welcome to Stroessnerplatz, gentlemen.''

Ted recognized the sixty-three-year-old general from pictures sent over by Senator Mason. The stocky ex-military figure was dressed in a sport shirt and trousers. His hair and mustache had turned dark gray.

"I'm Ted Taylor, and this is my cousin, Bernard Taylor. We've been anxious to meet you."

"The sentiment is mutual, I assure you. Sit down." He indicated a love seat.

They'd been brought to a home, quite an elegant one if this living room with its ornate moldings and grand piano was anything to go by. Someone with wealth had been the original owner. Von Haase?

Ted noticed that the general walked with a slight limp as he made his way to a chair and waved his guards off.

"Would you care for something to drink?"

They both declined. "We never drink on a job this important."

The general studied them at length. "That is very commendable. Dr. Arbizu has given me the details I requested. Your backgrounds have been checked and are impeccable. My congratulations. It appears you have the ear of the president of the United States himself. At this point, I have to ask why you would be willing to pay such an exorbitant amount to back someone as insignificant as myself when I can offer no proof that I will be successful."

"We're bankers. We back many ventures that are not successful. But we back many more that are." Bernard sat forward. "We are hoping that when you become president of Paraguay, you will open your doors to Global Banking."

He continued his well-rehearsed speech. "The current president of your country has put a moratorium on any more foreign banking interests within its borders. We wish to extend our influence abroad, particularly here in South America. We believe it's the continent of the future.''

"We've been biding our time, waiting for the winds of change to blow here,'' Ted inserted. ''Sometimes an unexpected act of nature can stir them up a little. We're patient men.''

The general smiled. ''All right. You've convinced me. But let us talk about the bottom line, as you Americans say. You know as well as I do that my next military campaign could end in failure. What is it you want for collateral?''

Ted's heart began to race like a runaway train. He and Bernard had talked it over and decided to take the gamble.

''Because Global Banking is a leader in the world banking community, Nazi hunters have been working with us to investigate money trails worth billions of dollars in gold and assets.

''Certain information has come to light from a U.S. Senate probe into the covert activities of U.S. Navy-trained SEALs on special assignment in Paraguay.''

Thank God for Jordan and Stoney. Ted couldn't have come up with a convincing enough source otherwise, one the general would verify through his own home network.

''They have given testimony of positive proof that Gerhardt von Haase has been living at Stroessnerplatz for at least forty-five years, maybe longer, funding past operations such as yours in exchange for protection.

"Since the probe findings were reported, we've talked personally with Nazi hunters out of Switzerland, Canada and Israel who've been on von Haase's trail for years now and are privy to that classified information.

"As we speak, they are gathering interested parties who will remain nameless to invade Stroessnerplatz for the express purpose of arresting him, with or without your president's permission or yours."

The general didn't move. That could mean anything.

"Forewarned is forearmed, as they say." Bernard picked up where Ted had left off. "Naturally my cousin and I don't wish to see you and your army destroyed before you can attempt another coup. In any event, we can't take the risk of Global Banking being exposed.

"If word reached the president of the United States of our connection with you, we could be brought up on international conspiracy charges and sent to prison.

"You ask about collateral? It is this—you hand von Haase over to us and he will be taken to the proper authorities in Israel. When word gets out that the Vampire of Alsace has been found and will stand trial for his crimes, Stroessnerplatz will no longer be a target.

"Those in power both in and out of Paraguay know this is the stronghold of General Oriana. They will see you in a more favorable light because you gave up one of the world's most notorious criminals. It's a gesture that will bode well for your political future, both domestically and internationally.''

Ted took over again. "Once he is gone, you will be free to plan your strategies without fear of trouble from outside sources," he said. "If you should manage to overthrow the present regime, then we're all winners. If you don't, then it's a risk that didn't pay off.''

"When you are ready to give up von Haase, we will bring five million dollars' worth of guaraníes to the compound. After you are president of the country, we will pay five million more to help you through the transition period."

"You don't have to make a decision tonight. Sleep on it. Ask Dr. Arbizu to contact us when you have an answer. We will be in Asunción for the next four days. That should be enough time for you to consider things carefully. If we don't hear from him before we leave, then we will know why your first coup attempt failed.''

"Why is that?" the general inquired in a less cordial tone than before. Bernard had found a small chink in Oriana's armor.

"It's obvious. Von Haase's cash reserves finally ran out, and you couldn't find another backer you could trust. But a little faith precedes the miracle. If you will instruct one of your guards to bring in the doctor's bag from the back of the van, you will find another fifty thousand dollars' worth of guaraníes as a further gesture of our goodwill.''

After a few seconds the general cocked his head. "How do I know you're not really Nazi hunters trying to do what all the others before you have attempted without success?''

"You don't," Ted retorted with a wintry smile. "It's possible my cousin and I could be the first ones to alight from an Israeli commando helicopter when they invade your compound.''

"On the other hand—" Bernard followed Ted's lead "—how do we know you won't take our untraceable money and skip the country, leaving us poorer than before, and still unable to do banking business in Paraguay?''

The older man rubbed his mustache back and forth. "You two are more clever than the rest.''

"The fact that you, General, have survived your first coup attempt and are preparing to stage another without the necessary funds speaks volumes.

"Now, if you don't mind, we're very tired after our flight from the States and would like to return to our hotel.''

To Ted's surprise the general threw back his head and he laughed. "I like you.''

You like our money, you low-life bastard.

Now it's a waiting game to see just how much.

"What if, hypothetically, I were to produce von Haase, and you decide he's not the genuine article?''

"We will know.'' *We* will *know. It'll be like looking in a distorted mirror.*

"Time has a way of altering people. You could retaliate by saying I'd tricked you."

Ted shrugged his shoulders negligently. "You could shoot us before we leave the compound and lose out on ten million dollars. To get back to the issue, DNA tests aren't affected by age. With the good doctor's help, blood can be drawn.

"Rest assured we will be satisfied it is von Haase before we continue negotiations. We're bankers, not assassins."

"DNA tests would be pointless. Von Haase's family did not survive the war."

Their grandfather was here. Ted had to fight his euphoria. He didn't dare look at his cousin.

"Then von Haase lied to you, General."

For the first time since their conversation began, the older man's hands trembled.

CHAPTER TWELVE

"THANKS FOR ANOTHER delicious meal, Mary. You've spoiled me outrageously while I've been staying here. My doctor will have a fit when I go in for my next appointment and he tells me I've gained fifty pounds."

"From where I'm sitting, you look mighty fine." Jordan's green eyes were smiling.

"Don't I though?" Deborah quipped. "Problem is, I'm so large I can't get close to the table like the rest of you."

"Watch your mouth, Jordan. One of these days Rickie's going to have the same problem, and it'll be your fault."

While Rickie shook her head in exasperation, Jordan's laughter resounded in the Quonset hut's kitchen. "Where did you get an idea like that, Mary?"

"I think Stoney'll be flying in any minute now." The older woman got up from the table, avoiding another of Jordan's questions. The friendly banter between the two of them left Deborah in a constant state of amusement.

"He'll be hungrier than a bear in springtime

'cause he left without eating his breakfast. I'd better get his lunch warmed up,'' she mumbled.

Deborah loved being over here with everybody. They'd put her to work teaching English to the Indian families. Since English hadn't been Deborah's first language, either, she had a better understanding of how to go about assisting them.

It had been a delightful experience, and had helped fill the empty hours. Otherwise she couldn't have stood the separation from Ted.

Jordan's voice broke into her thoughts. "What time is Ted due in today?"

Deborah's gaze flicked back to him. "Sometime this evening. He'll call and let me know. In the meantime, I need to go home and get a few things done so I'll be ready to pick him up."

"I don't want to let you go," Rickie said. "It's been wonderful having you here."

"I've enjoyed it so much. If it's all right with you, I'd like to spend a couple of days here every week."

"You know how much you're needed and wanted. The apartment is always available. Just make sure it's all right with my brother. I don't want him thinking we coerced you into anything."

"Of course he won't think that. Now I'd really better go."

"I'll walk you out," Jordan offered. "Where's your suitcase?"

"It's the tan overnight bag. I put it by the front door."

They got up from the table. Deborah cleared her

place and took the dishes to the sink. After giving Mary and Rickie a hug, she followed Jordan out of the hut.

When they reached her car and he'd put the bag inside, she turned to him and put a hand on his arm. "Could we talk for a minute?"

Her tone must have alerted him that something was wrong. His expression sobered. "Of course."

Her mouth had gone dry. It was impossible to know how he felt about discussing Rickie's parents, since the subject had never come up. But he was her brother-in-law and they'd grown closer in the past week. She trusted him implicitly.

"Jordan, no one knows what I'm about to tell you. Not Rickie, and especially not Ted."

"Go on," he urged quietly.

"I went to Graycliff last Monday to see my new in-laws."

He blinked. "I thought they were in Japan."

"They are, but I caught them before they left. I went to see them for answers."

"Answers?" He looked puzzled.

"Yes. Ted is suffering from something horrible, something he won't talk about. I know now that whatever caused his trauma, was also the reason he broke off our engagement.

"I always felt that his relationship with his parents held the key to his problems. This was proved to me conclusively this morning, when I met them. Jordan, those people are dead inside. And they've made Ted the way he is. On the night of our wedding...'' She faltered for a moment. "On the night of our wedding,'' she began again, "while we were exchanging gifts, I saw this awful grief in his eyes. I've seen it too many times before. It changes him into someone else. Someone I don't know.''

For the next few minutes, Deborah explained about the watch and her husband's devastating behavior. "I'm convinced there's a family secret that's slowly destroying him. Because you're married to Rickie, I thought you might know what his reaction was all about.''

She tried to keep the tremor out of her voice but failed miserably. "I guess what I'm asking you for is confirmation that this isn't a figment of my imagination.''

He expelled his breath; she felt his strong arms go around her. He held her for a few minutes. "You're not losing your mind, Deborah. I don't have answers. I only know the Taylor family is in pain.''

"It's obvious that Ted and Rickie's parents love them. What could have happened that was so terrible, it prevented them from giving their children what they needed?''

"Maybe one day the answer will come out.''

"I was hoping Rickie might shed some light.''

For a moment his arms seemed to tighten. "There are still things she can't talk about.''

"I'm sorry.'' She clung to him. "It must be hard for you, too.''

"Rickie's farther along the road to recovery than Ted."

"I can tell. She's not the same person who came to visit our family in Jerusalem early this year. You've made her the happiest woman on earth."

He slowly relinquished his hold on her. "Those words mean a lot coming from you, but I could have sworn *you* were that woman."

She averted her eyes. "I—I would be if I thought Ted could put the pain behind him."

"Don't give up hope, Deborah. Every day Rickie lets go of her ghosts a little more. That's what Ted is doing—or he wouldn't have come back for you and the baby."

"I want to believe that."

"Then believe it. Trust in it. From my viewpoint, he's already a changed man. Ted's been calling you day and night. It's a miracle anybody got anything done around here." He winked.

Ted had called her a lot while he'd been away, more than she'd expected. His attentiveness had thrilled her.

"I'll never forget the look of joy on his face when he proclaimed in front of everyone, 'You're my wife now!'"

She smiled in spite of her fears. "I won't, either."

"The man's crazy about you, Deborah. Let that be enough. The future will take care of itself."

"Rickie's a very blessed woman."

His eyes softened. "The four of us are blessed to have found each other."

"I agree. See you next week."

He helped her into the car and shut the door. "Drive carefully. You've got precious cargo."

I do.

She waved to him before heading home. By evening she'd be in Ted's arms. She could hardly breathe just thinking about it.

TED HAD JUST given the taxi driver instructions to head for Asunción's airport when the cell phone rang. That had to be the call from Arbizu. "There's nothing like leaving it until the last second," he muttered.

They'd spent the last four days planning von Haase's removal from Paraguay. Every step, including a passport with Paraguayan entry stamp, had been worked out in detail, but the waiting had been hell.

"He doesn't know how to play any other kind of game," Bernard said before he answered.

The conversation lasted all of one minute. When he'd clicked off the phone, he turned to Ted. "The general has made his decision. He's ordered Arbizu back to the compound to draw blood. We're to pick it up at the hospital in the morning. He went for it!"

Ted echoed his cousin's elation. "That bastard doesn't believe we have the proof. He's in for a big shock, but I must admit he's more shrewd than I gave him credit for."

"I think it's a case of his being more frightened," Bernard responded. "You scared the hell out of him when you mentioned that commando helicopter. He had no way of knowing if you were bluffing or not." He leaned toward the front seat and gave the driver revised directions. They'd be staying in Asunción another night.

Ted smiled. "We can put a rush on those tests and have results in seven days."

"Hold on. It might take longer. He's made a stipulation."

"What?"

"He's insisting that the testing be done at the Berthier Medical Center in Neuchâtel, Switzerland."

"How in the hell does he have a connection there?"

"A colleague of Arbizu's works in the lab at Berthier."

Ted's thoughts raced ahead. "As long as his contact will be faxing the results to Arbizu, we might as well order our own tests from the clinic in Poughkeepsie. It won't hurt to provide two sets of DNA results when we hand over von Haase to the authorities."

"In spite of everything, you know Oriana is going to give us the wrong man when we make the exchange."

"Of course. He'll force Arbizu to lie through his teeth. But the general won't get one cent of his first five million unless he shows up with the real von Haase. Since we're the only ones who can make positive visual identification, that part of our plan is foolproof."

"You don't trust him any more than I do."

Ted shook his head. "No, I don't. But keep in mind that we have no idea what shape our grandfather's going to be in."

"We know he's not dead or the general wouldn't go through the motions of drawing blood. But even if von Haase is dying, I want his last gasp to be heard by Israelis on Israeli soil."

I want him a lot more alive than that!

A few minutes later, the taxi pulled up in front of a different hotel. Ted got out of the back seat and followed Bernard inside. With luggage in hand, they approached the desk and were given keys to their new accommodations.

"I'm going to go on up and call Deborah."

"While you do that, I'll order us a couple of drinks from the bar, then join you."

Thankful for the privacy, he hurried to their room. Deborah wouldn't be any more disappointed than he was over the change in plans.

As soon as he'd locked the door, he called her on the room phone. She picked up after the first ring.

"Hello?"

Every time he heard her voice, it was like the first time. "Darling?" He stopped pacing. "You sound out of breath."

"Ted, I'm so glad it's you. I just walked in the house to get ready to pick you up. How soon does your plane get in?"

He rubbed the back of his neck. "I'm afraid an important business matter has arisen and we won't be able to make it until tomorrow afternoon around five.''

"Oh, no.''

"If it wasn't vital, nothing would have delayed me, Deborah. As I told you earlier, we've been scouting new locations in Switzerland to expand our facilities. This one in Neuchâtel looks promising. We need to look into it a little more.''

Another lie.

A long silence, then "I understand.''

"If I were in your place, I wouldn't understand at all,'' he said bitterly. "It's hell being separated from you like this.''

"I admit I'm disappointed, but that's business. Just hurry home tomorrow.''

"You know I will.'' *There won't be any more lies after we take care of von Haase. I can promise you that, my love.* "What are you going to do until bedtime?''

"Start on the baby book. There's a lot of information I can fill in now about you and me. How we met and where. When we got married. Our feelings about having the baby. I thought I'd get that part done before he arrives.

"The other day I bought one of those calligraphy pens to make the writing look more professional. Even so, it takes some practice to get the strokes right.''

He'd seen the book. There was a whole page on the family tree with spaces to put photos of the baby, his parents, grandparents and great-grandparents.

She already had a box full of family heirlooms supplied by the Solomons. Deborah knew her family history backward and forward.

One day soon she would ask him for his parents' family album so she could duplicate the pictures and information. Not only the Taylor background, but that of the Jessops, a fictitious English line created for his German mother's side of the family. It would all be lies.

His body broke out in a cold sweat.

"Ted? Darling?"

His head jerked guiltily. "Yes?"

"You're obviously preoccupied. I'm going to let you go."

"Deborah…" Her voice sounded so hurt.

"It's all right, Ted. Call me tomorrow when you know the time of your arrival. I love you."

"I love you. When I get you alone, you'll find out how much."

TWO DAYS LATER, Ted was in his office, staring at his computer screen.

"Mr. Taylor?"

"Yes, Alice?"

"Your father's secretary just phoned me back and said he's free right now if you want to see him."

"Thank you. I'm going to be out of the office for a few hours. Please hold all my calls."

"What about your wife?"

"She can always reach me on my cell phone."

"Oh, of course. Yes, sir."

Since his return from Paraguay, things hadn't been the same between them. Deborah tried to pretend everything was normal. Her response in bed was everything he could hope for. But she couldn't hide the sadness in her eyes at odd moments when she didn't think he was looking.

He knew that during their last phone conversation from his hotel room in Asunción, he'd failed her when he hadn't wanted to talk about the baby book.

Bernard had warned him to be careful, or his alienation from their unborn child could jeopardize his marriage. On an intellectual level Ted understood what his cousin meant. But emotionally, he wasn't capable of manufacturing feelings that didn't exist.

Could any man be thrilled to know he'd spawned another von Haase with the genetic potential to wield demonic evil on an unsuspecting world?

Ted left his suite of offices and used the staircase to the top floor occupied by his father and uncle. Unless it was a matter of necessity, he preferred not to see his father at all.

Though still the titular heads of Global Banking, Alexander and John Taylor had turned over the bulk of the work to their sons. Out of town most of the time these days, they only served the board in an advisory capacity. Ted and Bernard were the ones who ran the organization.

The day would soon come when their fathers would step down and relinquish all claim. When that moment occurred, Global Banking, along with all its attendant investments, would cease to exist.

Every facility would be sold, every holding would be liquidated. Ted and his cousin would give every employee a year's severance pay.

All the cash proceeds would be equally divided among as many surviving Jewish families as could be traced to the names on the records kept by von Haase and ultimately confiscated by the Allies after the war.

It would take a lifetime of work, but he and Bernard would see that their plan was carried out, even after their own deaths.

The child Deborah was carrying would have to identify with the Solomon side of the family. His grandfather Benjamin would be the perfect role model. Ted would make sure their son spent as much time in Jerusalem as possible.

Through Ben's wisdom, his grandson would learn how to really live. He would be taught how to earn an honorable living, how to make his own way in the world.

Ted refused to allow the child resulting from his own corrupt body even the remotest possibility of inheriting blood money. Such ignominy needed to be obliterated from the earth.

"Ted? Are you all right?"

At the sound of Neta's voice, Ted stopped mid-stride to greet his father's secretary.

"Sorry. I had a lot on my mind. Didn't see you."

"Just between you and me, you do the work of

ten men in one day. That couldn't be good for a new marriage."

"I appreciate your concern. Don't worry. I have plans to rectify the situation." *Plans that will force you out of a job, but you'll be well compensated.*

He entered his father's office, shutting the door behind him.

"Neta said you were on your way up." His father stood by the window looking out at the view. He could never deal with Ted eye to eye. That refusal to meet his son halfway had always devastated Ted.

Learning that his father was one of von Haase's unfortunate offspring went a long way to explain the painful deficiency. Ted understood Alexander's shame better than any man alive could possibly understand it.

What he couldn't forgive was his father's inability to talk about it, to lift one finger to erase it. All these years he and Ted's mother had kept their hideous secret by running away every chance they got. They'd never once considered that their flight from pain would be so detrimental to their own children.

We weren't a family. We were four people under one roof, living private lives of agony.

"If you're free for lunch, I'd like you to do me a favor." It was the only favor he'd ever asked of his father. The shock brought Alexander's head around.

"When Aunt Elizabeth was dying, she required quite a few blood transfusions. The family was supposed to replenish the supply, but the request was overlooked. Now the blood bank at the hospital is running low.

"Bernard called a little while ago and asked if you and I would meet him and Uncle John there to donate a pint each. I figure it's the least we can do for the cause. What do you say?"

"Of course" came the quiet reply. "I had no idea."

"Neither did I. The transfusions couldn't keep her alive, but our blood might help extend someone else's life."

Your blood, my dear father, is going to pave the way for the trial of the century.

"Just a minute while I tell Neta I'm going to be out of the office for a few hours."

Bernard's ingenious idea had worked like a charm, putting Ted in a much better frame of mind than before. But his father's next words as they stood in front of the elevator doors shattered whatever pleasure he'd been taking in the moment.

"Your wife came to visit us last week."

The blood pounded in his ears.

So that was what Deborah had been doing on the day of her doctor's appointment.

Ted distinctly remembered how vague she'd been about her activities.

Had she even gone to see her obstetrician?

The elevator arrived and they stepped inside.

"I assumed she would have told you. Your mother and I thought her very lovely."

Why did you do it, Deborah? Why did you go there?

"Deborah told us you two are expecting a baby. I didn't realize it was going to be so soon. Late December, I believe she said."

Has it come to this already, my love? Now you're keeping secrets from me?

"She's worried about you, Ted."

Dear God.

"Is there anything I can do?"

As the doors opened to the underground car park, Ted felt the white heat of rage consume him.

"After thirty years of silence, I didn't know a question like that was even part of your vocabulary. I'll bring my car around."

"DEBORAH?"

Ted? Her heart raced with excitement.

It was only midafternoon. Had he felt the tension between them and decided to come home early and talk things out? She'd been praying his mood would change.

"I'm in the nursery, darling."

She put down the curtains, ready to run into his arms, but he stopped at the doorway. There was an enigmatic look in his eyes. It prevented her from reaching out to him.

"What's wrong?"

"We've hit a snag in negotiations for the Neuchâtel property. I have to fly back to Switzerland."

"Now?"

"Yes. I came home long enough to put a few things in a case and leave for the airport. Bernard's swinging by to pick me up. We should be back tomorrow or the next day. I'll let you know."

Disappointment caused her heart to plummet. Before he left, she had to at least try to find out what was causing this hostility. She'd never seen him like this. It frightened her as much as the awful sadness that sent him into a black state of depression.

"Let me help you." She hurried down the hall and followed him to their bedroom.

He moved too fast for her. In the brief moment after he discarded the shirt he'd worn to work in preference for a clean one, she glimpsed a plaster strip on the crook of his inner arm. It hadn't been there earlier.

"What happened to your arm?"

"I, uh, nicked the skin with the letter opener. Alice fixed me up."

"You should have a tetanus shot."

"You're beginning to sound like a wife." His remark stung, as it was meant to do.

He pulled his overnight bag and a suit from the closet and threw them both on the bed. Before she could reach his dresser, he'd found a shirt and tie he wanted. In a few deft movements he had everything packed.

She took a fortifying breath. "Ted—you can't go away like this."

"Like what?" he called from the bathroom.

"You're angry about something. If I'm to blame, then let's talk it out. Please."

"I don't have time." His words cut like a knife.

"What have I done? Tell me so I can fix it." This was a side of Ted she'd never encountered.

He put his toiletries in a zippered bag and packed it with his clothes before he shut the case. "What I'm talking about can't be fixed." When he lifted his head, she saw that his gaze had turned wintry. A part of her heart seemed to shrivel.

He must mean the baby.

He loved her, but he'd never intended her to get pregnant. There'd been no pretense about his lack of excitement over the coming event. Now that her due date was drawing close, it was increasingly clear that he dreaded the idea of becoming a father.

"Would you rather I went back to Jerusalem until after the baby's born? I've had a lot longer than you have to get used to the idea that I'm going to be a mother. I—I think maybe you need some time alone. I can leave on the next plane."

He'd grabbed his suitcase and had started to walk out, but her words brought him to a halt. Without looking at her he said, "That's the last thing I want. Would you want to shame me before your parents?"

Another stab wound. She swallowed hard.

"I made a commitment to you, Deborah. I just wish you'd kept your promise to me."

She shook her head in agony. "What promise?"

"To stay away from my parents until I felt the time was right to introduce you. No power or person can put me and my family back together. Not even you.'' His voice was cold.

The back of her wrist went to her mouth in a reflex action. *His parents.* He must have talked with them earlier in the day.

''I was going to tell you about that visit, but...but you seemed so preoccupied with business. I would have told you tonight, darling. I swear it.''

''I believe you.'' She could see his chest heaving. ''There's Bernard. I have to go.''

''Forgive me.'' She was devastated. ''I'll never go behind your back again.''

''Don't make promises you can't keep.'' He turned away. ''I'll lock the door on my way out.''

CHAPTER THIRTEEN

WITH A PAIN too deep for tears, she dashed to the window and watched him leave the house to join Bernard.

You're slipping away from me, Ted. What am I going to do?

When she couldn't see the Mercedes any longer, she rushed to the baby's dresser where she'd put her cell phone, and punched in Rickie's phone number.

Be there, Rickie.

"Stoney's Air Cargo. Mary Moe speaking."

"Mary? It's Deborah."

"Hi, honey. How are you and the half-pint doing?"

After the chilling scene with Ted, the warmth in Mary's voice opened the floodgates. "We're all right."

"Doesn't sound that way to me."

"Is Rickie there?"

"No. She and Jordan went out with some of the children earlier. I expect them back in time for dinner. Can I give them a message?"

"No— Yes— Tell them I need to talk to them. I'm going to drive over there as soon I can get ready."

"You do that. It'll make everyone's day. I'll set another place at the table. Drive carefully now."

"I will. Thank you, Mary."

It didn't take Deborah long to throw a nightgown, maternity pants, a couple of tops and some toiletries in her overnight bag. Throughout her preparations, she kept worrying about Ted's arm.

She supposed an accident like he'd described might have happened, but for some reason she suspected he might have been to see a doctor.

Maybe something really was wrong with him. Her thoughts flashed back to that night in Jerusalem when she'd phoned Bernard to ask him if Ted was dying.

At the time both Bernard and Ted had allayed her fears, but what if they'd been lying to her? His anger a few minutes ago could have been a smoke screen for something much more serious than her innocent visit to Graycliff.

On impulse she looked for Alice's extension in her little address book and punched in the numbers on the cellular phone.

"You've reached Theodore Taylor's office. Alice Gatlin speaking."

"Alice? It's Deborah Taylor."

"Hello! I'm afraid you've just missed your husband."

"Don't worry. He came home before leaving for Switzerland." Her voice trembled despite her resolve.

"Oh, good. What can I do for you? Did he forget something?"

"No. Actually, I wanted to thank you for taking such good care of him today."

The older woman laughed. "If he said that, then it's news to me. He was only in the office for an hour this morning. Not even long enough to ask me to send out for coffee and doughnuts."

By now Deborah was starting to feel panicky. "He hurt his arm. I just assumed you were the one who gave him first aid."

"No," she answered thoughtfully. "But he and Bernard went out to lunch with the senior Taylors today."

Now I know how Ted found out.

"Maybe the two of them stopped for a game of handball afterward. Occasionally they'll return to work sporting a cut or a bruise. They both have a competitive spirit, but I guess I don't have to tell you that."

It was odd, but Deborah had never thought of Ted and Bernard in that light. Quite the opposite, in fact.

"No," she lied.

"Don't worry about your husband. You know men, they'd rather die than admit anything's wrong."

She nodded and wiped her eyes. "You're right. Forgive me for bothering you."

"Oh, heavens. It's wonderful to talk to you. Call anytime."

"Thank you, Alice."

Though only an hour and a half had passed before she reached Stoney's place, Deborah had to wait two more hours before Rickie and Jordan arrived. Mary always seemed to know how to help. She put Deborah to work peeling vegetables. It kept her hands occupied, and the mundane, repetitive task was actually rather soothing.

When Rickie finally came through the front door, she took one look at Deborah's face and insisted she follow her to the apartment in the other hut, where Deborah stayed.

"Mary phoned us while we were in town and told us you were so upset, you were on your way over to see us. We got back as soon as we could. What's wrong? Where's Ted?"

Jordan had pulled up a chair for Deborah before looping an arm around his wife as they sat on the bed.

"He left for Switzerland with Bernard."

Rickie frowned. "Again?"

"Does it really surprise you?" Deborah blurted.

Both of them looked puzzled. Jordan spoke first. "What do you mean?"

Deborah couldn't stay seated. "I'm going to ask you the same question I asked Bernard several weeks before the wedding. I—Is Ted dying?"

"Deborah!" Rickie cried out in unfeigned shock. "What would make you think that?"

Her reaction seemed so genuine, Deborah almost wished she hadn't asked the question. But she was desperate for answers.

"Although I can't prove it, I'm pretty sure Ted saw a doctor today. He pretended he'd hurt his arm at the office and Alice had fixed him up, but I called her and found out she didn't know anything about it."

"Did he have bruises on his arms? Sometimes he gets them playing handball."

Deborah shook her head, then explained what she'd seen. "If he's terminally ill, it could explain the reason he's had blood drawn. Do you think he could be consulting a specialist in Switzerland? Please," she beseeched them, "if you know anything at all, tell me. At this point I swear the secrets are harder on me than the truth would be."

Rickie stood up and grasped Deborah's hands. "If Ted has a mysterious illness, I know nothing about it. I swear it."

"It would be news to me, too," Jordan assured her.

They both sounded too sincere to be lying.

Deborah shuddered. "Then it's the baby that's making him sick. He doesn't want it, but he's promised to be a good father. He's tried so hard to do everything right, but the conflict is killing him."

Rickie looked as horrified as Deborah felt.

"I told Ted I'd go back to Jerusalem until after my delivery, but he wouldn't hear of it because he's afraid of disappointing my parents. Would you two mind if I stayed here like I did before? I'll pay my own expenses. I can help Mary with the meals and continue teaching English to the families."

"Forget the money," Jordan said with uncharacteristic sharpness. "It's a given that you can always stay here. We're thankful for the help."

"Stoney might not approve."

"Stoney's not the problem. You know he's crazy about you. I'm just afraid that when Ted finds out, he's not going to be pleased."

She stared at Jordan. "He's not pleased about anything these days. But at least he'll have his space. With the news of the baby thrust on him like that, I'm convinced solitude is what he needs. He's been a bachelor for a long time."

"The pregnancy came as a surprise to you, too," Rickie reminded her. "He should be thinking about *your* needs right now."

"Please don't be upset with him, Rickie. He's angry at your parents. I've figured that much out. You survived your childhood with fewer emotional scars than Ted. Maybe he's one of those people who'll never be able to overcome the pain. If that's true, then our marriage is doomed."

Rickie's face lost its color. "Don't say that."

"I'm not giving up yet. But if things continue like this after the baby's born, there won't be a marriage to salvage. He won't like it, but he'll have no choice except to let me return to Jerusalem. I refuse to raise our son in a home filled with pain—like yours was. It would be history repeating itself."

Jordan pulled her into his arms. "Why don't you take this thing one day at a time and see what happens?"

Deborah clung to him. "I want to. I love him more than life. But please don't tell me again that he feels the same way about me. Even if it's true, he isn't capable of rising above his grief."

Neither he nor Rickie said another word as the three of them walked over to the other hut for dinner. Deborah appreciated their silence, but because they no longer tried as hard to convince her she was wrong, her despair had grown a little deeper.

As BERNARD BACKED out of the driveway, Ted hurried up the steps of the house with luggage in one hand, flowers and Swiss chocolate in the other.

He'd been gone two days. In that time, he hadn't called his wife, nor she him. He knew the pain he'd inflicted on Deborah couldn't be justified or remedied by an unsatisfactory apology over the phone. In any event, he and Bernard had needed to concentrate on getting the DNA testing set up.

The gifts had been the last-minute gesture of a desperate man. But knowing Deborah, it might have been better if he'd returned empty-handed.

Though she wouldn't throw his olive branch back in his face, she would in all probability ignore the time-honored symbols of contrition. Her quiet rejection would increase his guilt a hundredfold.

Still, he had to do something.

He rang the doorbell to alert her, then let himself in and called her name.

When there was no answer, he made a tour of the house, starting with the kitchen. Every room was spotless and empty. There was no note explaining her absence, no voice mail message.

She could be out doing errands, but he had a gut feeling, she'd gone to Stoney's place for solace.

A phone call confirmed his suspicions. Mary said she and Rickie were out shopping for groceries and would be back soon. He thanked Mary for the information, then asked her not to tell Deborah he'd called. He wanted the element of surprise on his side when he showed up in a little while.

After a shower and change of clothes, he headed for Stoney's. Nothing would be accomplished until he could bring Deborah home and they had unlimited time to talk things out.

When he arrived at the hangar forty-five minutes later and saw the Honda parked in front of Mary's hut, he went inside. His wife and his sister were in the kitchen putting their purchases away.

Deborah had blossomed in the last two weeks. He didn't think she should be doing that much stretching and bending.

"Why don't you two take a rest and I'll finish up."

Their heads swerved around in surprise. Rickie's accusing eyes had turned an Arctic blue. Deborah's brown eyes were dark with pain. All he'd done was bring her grief. His self-loathing reached new depths.

Rickie's mouth tightened. "No thanks. But I know your wife shouldn't be working this hard."

"I agree," he muttered. "Deborah? Will you come outside with me, please? We have to talk."

At first he thought she was going to ignore him because she put another couple of milk cartons in the refrigerator. But when she'd shut the door, she told Rickie she'd be back soon, then walked around the counter toward him. Her beautiful face held no expression at all. It frightened the hell out of him.

"You're right, Ted," she said woodenly. "We do have to talk. But not here."

"I'll follow you home."

"I'm not going anywhere. That's what I want to talk to you about. For privacy's sake we can sit in my car."

He held the door open to allow her to pass.

The brisk evening air bordered on chilly. Darkness would be upon them soon. This close to Thanksgiving, she ought to be wearing a coat.

When they'd both gone outside he shut the door. "I have no intention of carrying on an intimate conversation with my wife in a car—as if we were two runaway teens who had nowhere else to go."

She stopped walking and turned to him. "Then I guess we won't be having that talk, after all. You've wasted your time driving out here."

He felt the adrenaline kick in. "Don't do this, Deborah. You know me well enough to realize I've hated myself for behaving the way I did, that I need time to apologize and explain."

"If that's what you want to do, then my car's the most convenient place."

Lord. When her chin came up like that, it was a tangible warning that she couldn't be pushed any further.

"All right."

She took the initiative and got in the driver's side before he could help her. The only choice he had was to lever himself in the passenger seat and shut the door.

There has to be a way to reach her.

"Deborah." He leaned closer and slid his arm along the back of her seat. "I was wrong to be upset about your visit to Graycliff. There is no excuse for how I treated you the other day.

"When I told you I didn't want you going to your parents in Jerusalem, I might as well have put you in a straitjacket. What option did I leave you but to turn to Rickie?"

He ran his fingers up and down her satiny braid, needing to touch her. She didn't respond. The ache for her increased.

"I'm sorry, darling. I wish to God I could put back the clock and rewrite the sequence of events. Getting angry and walking out on you is the kind of thing that tears at the foundation of a marriage. I swear I'll never let it happen again. Please say you can forgive me."

"Forgiveness doesn't come into it," she answered, too calmly for his peace of mind. "You resent the baby. No," she said when he tried to deny it. "Let me finish.

"Intellectually you thought you could handle me

and marriage and a family all at the same time. But on an emotional level, you've discovered that you're not ready for the responsibility suddenly thrust upon you. Most men aren't. I see that more clearly than you know, Ted.''

Every time she came up with a reason to explain his behavior, it made perfect sense, yet was so far off the mark. He found it agonizing.

"You're wrong, Deborah. I would never have asked you to marry me again if I hadn't been prepared to embrace it all. Darling, the only reason I reacted in anger the other day was because I was afraid my parents would somehow hurt you.'' That was true enough.

She made a sound that could have signaled any emotion. "How could they hurt me?''

"The fact that you'd even ask that question means you have no comprehension of their capacity to inflict pain. I know what you're trying to do for the simple reason that I've loved you too long and understand you too well. But you defied my express wishes.

"You're one of those lucky people who comes from a close-knit family. You have no experience of any other kind, so you think the baby will somehow make the impossible happen and bring our family closer together.

"You can't comprehend our child not having a normal relationship with my parents. But they aren't your normal grandma and grandpa. They never will be. Never. Your mother and father are the only grandparents our child is ever going to know.

"When I found out you went to Graycliff, I suffered because I knew you'd come away from your visit feeling empty and rejected. I wanted to spare you that."

She stirred in the seat. "You've just described your own feelings, Ted. My experience with your parents was quite different and very illuminating.

"Talking with them proved to me that they love you, but that they're harboring a secret they've never been able to share.

"Whatever it is, that secret has made it impossible for your family to enjoy a normal life together. I don't know about Rickie, but I have a feeling you know what that secret is and it's slowly destroying you."

Dear God.

Early in his relationship with Deborah, her father had confided that she'd been named for the great Biblical judge and prophetess, Deborah.

When Ted had teasingly asked Ben if his daughter had ever exhibited those same remarkable abilities, the older man's expression had turned solemn and he'd simply nodded. For no accountable reason that look had sent chills down Ted's spine.

This time those same chills invaded every cell of his body.

"I'm sorry my parents did such a masterful job on you, Deborah. It seems you've come away with false notions they've planted in your mind—no doubt so you wouldn't think too badly of them.''

She jerked her head around to face him. In the fading light her body was a mere silhouette. ''No, Ted. They couldn't fake what I saw in their eyes before they even knew who I was. It was the same look of sorrow I've sometimes seen in yours. Except it's deadened them and I believe there's still life in you.

''Do you remember when I came to Rickie's reception? You stared right through me, not really seeing me at all. I had the impression you'd been given your own private tour of hell, and you couldn't rid yourself of its horrific images. Your parents' eyes held that look. It isn't something a person could fabricate. What human being would want to?''

Deborah, how could you possibly know so much when you know nothing?

''If you want the real reason I came over here, it was to get the truth out of Rickie and Jordan. You see, I called Alice to thank her for taking good care of you. That was another thing I did behind your back. She denied all knowledge of an injury.''

Oh, hell.

''Because of that bandage on your arm, I thought you and Bernard had lied to me in Jerusalem to cover up the fact that you're dying of an incurable disease. Your sudden trip to Switzerland convinced me you must be consulting a doctor there.''

With his emotions in chaos, Ted didn't think he could remain confined this way much longer. He needed to take her in his arms, make her pain go away. And his...

"But when I asked Rickie and Jordan," she continued, "they both swore to me that if you were terminally ill, they knew nothing about it." There was a pause. "I believed them. So, I put everything together and came to the conclusion that this terrible secret you and your parents are guarding prevents you from loving our child."

She faced straight ahead once more. "After giving this a great deal of thought, I've made the decision to stay here until the baby's born."

"You don't mean that!"

"You say you know me well, Ted. If that's true, then you know better than to think I would trifle with your feelings on a matter as important as this."

"I'm in love with you." He could hear the love. It ripped his guts out. "I've never denied it. I don't imagine those feelings will ever change. You're in my heart and soul forever. But I draw the line at risking our child's emotional health because you can't love him.

"To my mind, part of good prenatal care is the climate provided by the parents before delivery. This is a very happy time for me, joyful, in fact, as I anticipate my son's birth. But your family lies and your family secrets are taking their toll on that joy. The thought of separation is the only solution that brings me any peace."

Tears smarted his eyes. "Deborah—"

"Some fathers want to be in the delivery room to

experience the birth firsthand. I have no expectations where you're concerned, but I will let you bring me and the baby home from the hospital. Our son deserves to go to the place especially prepared for him, with both parents in residence. If you don't mind, Mom and Dad will be coming to visit us once he's born.''

He tried to swallow. ''You know I love your parents.''

''That's true, but they'd live with us for months if we let them. Mother intends to wait on me because that's how she is. She's counting the hours until she can get her hands on her first grandchild.

''I promise not to let them stay longer than a week. During that time my aunts will make an appearance, as well. That's as far into the future as I can foresee.''

She reached for the handle and opened the door. ''I'd move heaven and earth to take your pain away. But it's out of my hands, Ted. You're the only person who can do that.

''If you decide to tell me what's wrong before the baby's born, I'll come home to listen. Otherwise, I'll call you from the hospital.''

''For the love of God, Deborah! Are you telling me you don't want to see or talk to me for the next month?''

''Yes. I can't bear to see the grief in your eyes any more than you can bear to watch our baby grow inside me. We need a complete break from each other. That way I can be myself and so can you.

"You won't have to lie, or cover up your tracks with more lies, or defend your feelings, or your lack of them. You won't have to worry about what you say, or explain where you're flying to next or account for anything you're doing.

"As far as my checking up on you without your knowledge, have no fear. I'm through trying to figure out the impossible."

This is all going to be over with in a few weeks, darling. Just give me a little more time.

"Will you at least let me kiss you good-night?" He was close to begging.

"No. The second you touch me, I dissolve."

She was out of the car before he had the presence of mind to reach for her.

"COME IN AND let's talk, Deborah."

She sat down opposite Dr. Lambert's desk with some trepidation. During the examination he'd noted that her blood pressure was up a little, and that she seemed edgy.

Deborah feared he would want to discuss the reasons for the change in her condition. Since the scene in the car when she'd told Ted she wanted a separation, she'd cried herself to sleep every night.

She ached for him. The need to be with him, to lie in his arms, had grown acute. Too many times she'd broken down to the point that she'd almost run home to him.

Over the past two and a half weeks, she'd phoned Bernard often to make sure Ted was all right. She knew her husband had made constant calls to Rickie and Mary, checking up on her. But all of that was something she preferred to keep from her doctor.

"I'm not surprised you're having a lot of discomfort, Deborah. Either we've miscalculated the date of conception, or you're going to have this baby early."

She was stunned by the news. "How early?"

"Mid-December."

"Today's the second. That's only two weeks away!"

"Correct. The baby's head is down and he's dropped into position. I always said he was going to be a big one. If he's premature, he'll still be a good size. But assuming we're off on the date, that would explain why your measurements are larger than I would have expected at this time."

"Which do you think it is?"

"I'm not sure. This is your first. Did your mother go into labor prematurely?"

"No."

"Well, either way, you're about ready to deliver. I want to see you in a week. Don't take any trips, don't do any more driving than you can help, keep your feet up, stay away from salt and try to get as much sleep as you can.

"Phone me anytime. If your water breaks in the middle of the night, go to the emergency room. They'll call me and let me know what's happening."

Deborah thanked the doctor and left his office.

Under normal circumstances she would have headed right back to Stoney's. But because of the change in her due date, she drove to the house to pack some things, including the baby book, to take to the hospital with her.

While she was home, she'd write Ted a note telling him what the doctor had said. She would leave it on his dresser, where he'd be sure to see it.

Of course she'd also phone Bernard with the news so it could be conveyed to Ted, but it was important to her that her husband know she'd made a special effort to inform him.

She parked the car in front of the garage and let herself in the back door. It opened into a utility area, which led to the hallway connecting with the foyer.

The house looked and felt wonderful. Pain seared her heart that the tragic state of her marriage prevented her from living in it with the man she loved.

The more haunting thought—that she might never live here with him once the baby was a few weeks old—filled her with despair. But it was a reality she had to face.

If her husband had had any intention of baring his soul to her, he could have contacted her anytime in the last few weeks. She would have flown to him at a word.

But she'd listened for his phone call in vain. No matter how long and hard she'd prayed that he would open the hut door, he didn't appear. He'd made no the attempt to talk to her.

It was more than possible that in a month she'd

be flying back to Jerusalem. Her parents would welcome her and the baby until she could find a good apartment, but she knew they'd find it all distressing. Not only for the baby's sake, but for their own. They loved Ted.

So do I. Dear God, so do I.

Her heart breaking, she hurried toward the staircase, intent on getting her business done as quickly as possible. Too much time spent here, and she wouldn't be able to tear herself away.

As she put her hand on the carved banister to mount the stairs, Ted, dressed in the kind of conservative suit he usually wore to the office, began descending with two suitcases in hand. She'd had no idea he was here, in the house. They cried each other's names in stunned surprise.

With a swiftness she could barely countenance, he hurried the rest of the way. Dropping his cases, which skidded across the hardwood floors, he reached for her shoulders in a gesture as automatic as breathing. She couldn't tell whose body trembled harder.

His shadowed gaze roved over her features with a hunger she knew her eyes reciprocated. The handsome face she loved was drawn. He looked pale. She could tell he hadn't been eating regular meals.

"What are you doing here, darling? Why didn't you let me know you were coming?" He sounded out of breath.

"Would it have mattered if I had? You're obviously on your way to the airport again."

"Don't!" came his anguished cry.

He pulled her to him and his mouth descended. There was no thought of resistance. One brush of his fingers against her skin and it felt like a trail of fire burning its way through her body, consuming her.

Moaning, she gave in to the needs of her body and kissed him back. It had been so long and she wanted him so badly.

The baby made the kind of closeness she craved impossible, but it didn't stop either of them from rediscovering the other's eyes, nose, cheeks, throat, hands, mouth. Any part they could touch until the ritual began again with deeper, even more impassioned kisses.

Her braid came undone. The hair swirled about his hands and down her back. The sensation sent a rapturous warmth through her body. Until he'd placed her on their bed and slid next to her, it hadn't occurred to her that he'd carried her all the way upstairs.

Somewhere in the distance she heard the sound of a horn. But the reality of being with Ted like this made her realize how much she wanted and needed her husband, especially with the baby coming sooner than—

The baby.

"Ted," she murmured feverishly, remembering the reason she'd made a detour to the house in the first place. She cupped his face in her hands. "There's something I have to tell you."

"I know." The words came out as a half groan. "I heard Bernard honking, too. He'll just have to wait."

Bernard?

Of course. They're taking another trip. How could I forget a thing like that?

"You can't stand him up." She fought his mouth. "Besides, there's something important I have to tell you."

His hand stilled on her thigh.

"Dr. Lambert said the baby's coming sooner than we expected, probably in a couple of weeks. I came home to pack a bag for the hospital. I intended to leave you a note explaining everything."

He lifted his head a little higher and looked down at her with eyes the color of flint. "So you weren't coming back to me today."

I'm sorry, darling. Now you know how I've felt these past weeks. It's a living hell that goes on and on.

"No."

She sat up. The fact that he didn't try to stop her after what they'd been sharing signified that the magic had gone. Her pain returned with immobilizing force. Those moments they'd just experienced might never have happened.

By now he was on his feet pulling on the shirt lying next to the bed. With deft hands he tucked the hem in the waistband of his trousers, then shrugged into his suit jacket. "Two weeks, you say?"

She nodded. In a rush of words, she explained everything the doctor had told her.

Outside, Bernard was still honking. He must not have seen her car parked around the rear of the house or he would've stopped the noise and simply waited. His racket served to increase the tension between the two of them.

She watched her husband grab his tie, but he didn't put it on. "I don't know how long this trip to Switzerland is going to take, but I swear I'll be back before you go into labor. I intend to be there for the delivery. Take care, my love."

His hard mouth claimed hers one more time before he was out the door in a few swift strides.

DR. ARBIZU SIGNALED Ted to follow him down the hall of the general's house. Von Haase was supposedly being held in the back bedroom, where Ted would get his first look at his grandfather in the flesh.

He and Bernard had agreed to take turns sitting in the ambulance van to guard the five million dollars' worth of guaraníes.

As soon as Ted had seen enough, he would relieve his cousin so Bernard could get a thorough look at von Haase. If they were in agreement that the man was the genuine article, the trade would occur.

Dr. Arbizu had already assured the general that the money was all there in the van. The paper bills had been specially packed in the bottoms of medical cartons filled with blood plasma.

The private air-hospital jet they'd chartered for the trip to Paraguay housed a group of top-secret Israeli government authorities, doctors and a medical team. Disguised as medical workers, each held a phony American passport.

Once Ted and Bernard, dressed the same way, escorted von Haase aboard the plane, he would become the property of the Israeli government. Their people stood by ready to examine and interrogate him the second the doors of the plane closed and he was finally in custody.

This was the moment Ted and Bernard had been waiting for since the terrible truth of their German lineage had come to light.

If everything went as planned, the world would soon hear that the Vampire of Alsace had been captured and would stand trial for the role he'd played in the Holocaust.

On a more personal level, Ted would be able to face Deborah knowing he'd done something significant for the Jewish people, who deserved to confront one of their Nazi murderers.

Three days ago, he'd been forced to walk away from his grieving, pregnant wife with nothing resolved between them. It had happened too many times. He knew she was on the brink of leaving him for good, of going back to Jerusalem.

His life, his sanity, depended on the capture and exposure of von Haase. This close to the source of all his pain, Ted thought that if his heart pounded any harder, he might actually have a stroke. He took several deep breaths, willing his mind and body to achieve some semblance of calm.

The blood samples submitted to both the Poughkeepsie lab and the Berthier Medical Center in Neuchâtel for DNA testing had proven paternity beyond any doubt.

Both sides had satisfied the demands of the other. Oriana knew von Haase had living children, and Ted and Bernard knew Oriana had kept von Haase alive in Stroessnerplatz.

At least they had proof that their grandfather had been alive when the doctor had drawn the old man's blood. Now came the next test. To see if the general would try to pass someone else off as their monster relative.

"I've given him a sedative to keep him controlled during the transfer," the doctor whispered seconds before they passed two armed guards and he opened the door.

The accoutrements of the bedroom faded as Ted's eyes focused on the old man lying on top of a single bed, stretched out on his back.

He wore a clean, short-sleeved, yellow button-down shirt and white trousers with a woven straw belt and white shoes. Ted had seen a lot of men out on the country-club golf course who dressed like that.

Ted felt his chest constrict. He moved to the side

of the bed, studying the man's long legs, the shape of his large hands with their square-tipped fingers.

No doubt he'd shrunk in size, but Ted could tell that in his prime he would have been tall and rangy. His gaze continued to travel up the man's chest to his wrinkled neck, tanned and weathered by years in the hot sun. Though his jaw was slack, the same leathery skin was pulled taut over patrician cheekbones and a broad forehead.

A prominent nose jutted above thin lips, which he moistened from time to time. A wisp of silvery-gray hair covered the top and sides of his balding, tanned head.

Ted saw his father and uncle in the shape of the old man's receding hairline. His heart slammed into his ribs.

Blue eyes, dimmed by age, gazed up at him. Because of his drugged condition they showed no cognizance of where he was or what was going on, but their shape and color were unmistakable.

Taylor eyes. Von Haase eyes.

Oh my God, my God.

Ted looked with incredulity on the face and body of his grandfather, the man whose edicts had dehumanized thousands of terrified men, women and children before he'd slaughtered them.

Like a spectator at a horror film, Ted stared at this receptacle of flesh lying there so benign and subdued, while the ghastly pictures of torture and murder played through his mind.

If You're there, God—if there is a God—how

could You have allowed this miscreation to go on breathing the same air as the rest of us?

Should I be thanking You for preserving his life so he can answer to his victims' families for his crimes?

How can I bear his shame?

How did all those poor souls endure what he made them endure? Where did they find the courage?

How many hearts failed when their cries for help were never heard? And all because of this monster who looks like me.

"I've seen enough."

The doctor nodded and they left the room. Ted didn't remember the walk through the house to reach the outside, where the van stood parked.

As he approached, he saw Bernard get out on the driver's side. No words were necessary. Their eyes did the speaking. Bernard's body stilled in reaction before he turned on his heel and followed Arbizu into the house.

Ted took Bernard's place in the van, impatient to leave the compound and get in the air with their quarry. He wouldn't know elation until the moment the drug wore off and von Haase became fully aware of the nationality and destination of his captors.

It wasn't long before Bernard came out. Ted wasn't surprised at the brevity of his visit. One glimpse of their grandfather was all it had taken for either of them to verify the goods. Their eyes met again, this time in a private signal of satisfaction.

"Tell Oriana we're ready to make the trade at the perimeter gate. No blindfolds or handcuffs," Bernard dictated to Arbizu.

The doctor nodded, then returned to the house while Bernard climbed into the van to join Ted. By tacit agreement, neither of them spoke. It was as if they feared that saying the words aloud would somehow jinx their intricately laid plan.

He counted the seconds, breaking out in a new film of sweat. When Arbizu made another appearance and resumed his place behind the wheel, Ted felt relief pass through him and Bernard like a shock wave.

The general had given orders for a total blackout of Stroessnerplatz. Ted could see nothing more than the road illuminated by headlights as they wound their way through the compound to one of the gates.

"Remember our agreement," Ted said to the doctor. "The exchange takes place with the gates wide open."

Arbizu rapped out orders in Spanish and half a dozen armed guards leapt to do his bidding.

They waited another ten minutes in silence before Ted heard the sound of a truck slowing down behind them. Arbizu got out of the van. Ted followed Bernard out the other side.

He heard the scuffle of feet before more armed soldiers produced von Haase. He'd been strapped into a wheelchair. His head bobbed against his chest as they pushed him over the dirt.

How long had he been in a wheelchair? Or had Arbizu supplied one after sedating him?

While the boxes of money were hauled out of the van and carried to an older-vintage military transport truck, Ted and Bernard walked up to their grandfather and checked his pulse to satisfy themselves that he was still alive.

He was breathing. His flesh felt warm. But it was flesh like no other. Repulsed by that much contact, Ted quickly removed his hands. He noticed Bernard's fingers resisted touching him, too.

Once all the boxes were out, the two of them lifted him, wheelchair and all, and placed him in the back of the van.

"Not quite the honor cortege you expected for your funeral, is it, Grandfather?" Bernard's invective escaped with savage violence as they climbed inside with him and shut the doors.

The van's motor turned over and they were off.

How otherworldly it felt to be sitting here with their notorious grandfather at last.

"Aribzu shot him with enough drugs to make him borderline comatose."

Ted was furious about that, too. "For an eighty-nine-year-old man, he's in amazingly good shape."

Bernard put his face close to their grandfather's. "That's because your blood money allowed you to hide out and afford the best medical care. You monster! You bastard!"

Suddenly his cousin began sobbing.

It had been a long time in coming. Ted had wondered if Bernard's pain had gone so deep, if his cousin had reached an emotional cutoff point, a numbness, where no more feeling registered.

Ted sat back and closed his eyes.

Forty-five years the whole world had been looking for the fiend seated in the wheelchair next to him.

How sweet this private moment before the good news broke throughout Israel.

RICKIE WAS HOLDING Deborah's hand. Her sister-in-law hadn't left her side since she'd driven her to the hospital over fifteen hours ago.

It was nine days since the time the doctor had estimated her new due date. His words had been prophetic. Around seven this morning her labor had started.

It was Mary who'd called the doctor. On his orders, Rickie had driven Deborah to the hospital and taken care of everything.

She'd been in labor such a long time, the doctor recommended an epidural. Now, thanks to the medications, she was feeling no pain.

"Jordan is still doing everything possible to track Ted down."

"Don't worry about it. I told him before he left on this last trip that it would probably be two weeks at least. He had no idea I'd go into labor today."

Rickie's troubled blue eyes studied her intently. "He should never have gone away when he knew you were so close to your due date. His place is here with you. I'll never be able to forgive him for this."

"Don't be upset with him, Rickie. He's phoned me almost every day."

"That's not the same thing, and you know it. Here you are alone, so brave and strong, and loyal to him. He doesn't deserve you," she whispered.

Deborah shook her head. "Please. Don't you say it, too."

"What do you mean?"

"He tells me repeatedly that he's not good enough for me, that he's not worthy of me. I hate it when he says that." Tears streamed from her eyes.

Immediately contrite, Rickie handed Deborah some tissues. "I'm sorry for upsetting you. We won't talk about Ted again. If anyone can find him, Jordan can. In the meantime, we'll concentrate on you and your baby. The resident says you're fully dilated. It won't be long now."

"Did Mary reach my parents?"

"Yes. They'll be here on the next flight."

"That's good."

Deborah closed her eyes. *I thought I could do this without you, Ted. I thought I could. But I can't.*

Where are you, darling?

Please come home. I need you now.

"Well, Deborah?" Dr. Lambert came into the birthing room, followed by a team of nurses and the pediatrician. "This baby is ready to be born."

He smiled at Rickie. "Mrs. Browning? If you'll

go to the lounge, one of the nurses will let you know when you can come back in.''

Deborah felt Rickie's kiss on her forehead. ''Good luck, my dear, dear sister. I'll be praying for you.''

The next fifteen minutes passed in a blur as the doctor worked with Deborah and finally told her to bear down one more time. She did her best to co-operate, then heard an unmistakable gurgling sound that could only be her baby. Soon its newborn cries reverberated in the birthing room.

''Your little guy doesn't seem to like this cold, cruel world.''

Deborah's ecstatic cry mingled with her tears as Dr. Lambert laid the baby, with the umbilical cord still attached, across her stomach. Instantly the pain she'd been suffering over Ted's absence receded. In its place grew a welling of indescribable joy as she beheld their perfect child.

She raised her head as much as she could to get a good look at him. In a movement that reminded her of the unfurling of a leaf, he stretched his tiny limbs, which minutes before had been tightly wedged in the fetal position. He had a smattering of dark hair.

''He's beautiful.''

''He'll be even better looking when he's had his bath,'' the doctor teased.

''All I care about is that he's all right.''

''So far, everything looks fine.''

Relief overtook her exhausted body as the doctor

worked steadily to clear the baby's breathing passages, then cut the cord. Too soon he was handed over to the pediatrician, out of her sight.

"His color's good, Mrs. Taylor. So are his vital signs. He's breathing well." A minute later, she learned that he weighed in at eight pounds, two ounces, and was twenty-two and a half inches long.

Dr. Lambert's eyes smiled at her. "He's a good size. I think we were off on the date. When they've cleaned him up, they'll bring him back and you can inspect him to your heart's content."

"I can't wait."

"It won't be too much longer. In the meantime I'm almost through here, and I want you to get some rest. You're going to need it between feedings. He sounds hungry."

She felt a surge of elation. Her little boy was born. He was perfect.

When Ted sees him, his heart will melt. I know it will.

"HE'S GORGEOUS, Deborah."

"I think so, too, Mom."

"The last I saw of your father, he'd talked the nurse into letting him bathe the baby. So tell me while he's not here—what have you and Ted decided to name our grandson?"

Deborah turned away from her mother, who was sitting beside the hospital bed. "He left the decision up to me."

Her mother leaned forward. "And?"

"I—I don't know yet. I'm still thinking."

"Benjamin is a good name. So is Abraham."

"When Ted gets here, I'll ask him what he thinks."

"You do that. According to Rickie, he should be here any minute now. Don't get upset with him for something he couldn't help. Your father wasn't there for David's birth, either, because of the war, in fact he couldn't come home until two months later."

I know, Mother. I know the whole story and I've heard it a hundred times. I know you're trying to make me feel better, and I love you for it. But—

"Rickie said Ted's flight from Switzerland was delayed because of that hurricane close to the eastern seaboard."

I know that, too.

The call had come while Deborah was in the shower. Rickie had answered, but he'd rung off before she could hand the phone to Deborah. When Deborah had tried to call him back, he didn't answer.

With her emotions so near the surface, she didn't know how she would keep from bursting into tears when he finally arrived. The precarious state of their marriage had made her nervous about seeing him again.

Tomorrow morning she'd be going home. She had no idea how Ted would react to their son. To her.

She was afraid everything might be different now that the baby was born. Though she adored her parents and would forever be grateful to Rickie and Jordan and Mary, all she really craved was privacy with her husband and baby.

They needed time alone to sort things out. If there was anything *left* to sort out, her heart cried in anguish.

When her father entered the room a few minutes later, she suffered another disappointment; Ted still hadn't come.

"The nurse assured me she'll be bringing the baby in a few minutes. Try to be patient." He smiled and kissed her cheek before sitting down next to her mother to read the newspaper he'd brought with him.

Her poor parents didn't know anything was wrong. How long could she keep up this pretense in front of them?

"Miriam—Deborah—" An unexpected note of solemnity in her father's voice brought her head around. "You're not going to believe what's in the headlines."

"I heard there was another jet airliner crash over the Andes."

"That's tragic news, but this…" Her father was on his feet. The look in his dark eyes raised the hairs on the back of Deborah's neck.

He had her mother's full attention, as well. "What is it?"

"I'll read it to you." He shook his head. "This is incredible. Absolutely astounding. 'Nazi war criminal, Gerhardt von Haase, notorious Vampire of

Alsace, a main author of the Holocaust, has been found alive.'''

A stillness settled over the room as the three of them were forced to remember the unimaginable.

"Go on," her mother said, eyes vacant, no doubt thinking of the relatives whose lives had been extinguished at von Haase's death camp in Alsace.

Deborah hid her face in the pillow. She couldn't look at either of her parents, knowing that unbearable memories triggered their sorrow.

"'Nazi hunters picking up on his trail after forty-five years captured him in Paraguay. He has been bound over to the Israeli authorities. After the most exhaustive scrutiny, they have verified beyond any doubt that he is von Haase.

"'The Israeli people, overjoyed by the news, have delivered their mandate. They want him to stand trial immediately for his crimes. It is expected that as soon as doctors have declared him fit, a date will be set.'"

"Does it say how they found him?" Her mother asked the question with an excitement in her voice Deborah had never heard before.

"No. You know as well as I that they'd never release information of that nature. We should give thanks that he has finally been caught."

Even though the door to Deborah's room was partially open, there was a knock. She sat up as quickly as she could and looked around, hoping to see Ted.

Rickie came into the room.

She seemed hesitant, studying the three of them. "If this is a bad time—"

"No." Deborah shook her head. "Of course not. Dad was just reading us the headlines about Gerhardt von Haase's capture. You remember him from when we took you on that tour of the Holocaust museum? They've found him and turned him over for trial in Israel. It's amazing. It's the best news—"

Too late Deborah remembered how much her sister-in-law hated hearing anything to do with the Holocaust. "Dad! Quick— Help Rickie!" she cried.

Her father moved fast, catching Rickie around the waist. Her face had drained of color, leaving it an unhealthy white. Deborah's mother quickly stood so Rickie could sit down, then got her a drink of water.

"Thank you," she whispered. "I—I can't imagine why I reacted like that."

"His capture is going to affect millions of people the same way," Miriam mused aloud. "I'm sure he's too old to go on trial, but it doesn't matter. *He's been found.* We can all see him for ourselves one last time, say what we have to say, then put it to rest. This has to be one of the most liberating moments of my life."

Suddenly Rickie got to her feet. "If you'll excuse me, I need to phone Jordan to see when he's coming. I'll be right back."

Deborah noticed that her sister-in-law almost collided with the nurse who had brought the baby in for his feeding.

Still no sign of Ted.

The scene in the hospital room had taken on all the features of a strange dream. Too many emotions were pulling her in too many directions.

If it wasn't for her son, she wasn't sure how she was going to survive the next few hours, let alone the rest of her life.

BERNARD PULLED the car to a stop in the parking lot adjacent to the Poughkeepsie hospital. "You have to go in."

"It's the last thing I want to do."

"You told Rickie you were on your way. Deborah will be waiting."

"I don't think I can go through with this."

"So you're going to abandon her again? She's just had your baby!"

"It'll be better off never knowing me."

"Maybe you're right. But be a man this time," Bernard said brutally. "Tell her to her face. You owe her that much before you walk out for good. You made vows."

"That was a mistake."

"Then the hospital's the perfect place to say your goodbyes…before she goes home and you discover that she has expectations you can't meet. I'll go in with you and get rid of everyone else so you can be alone with her."

"I'm sick again, Bernard."

"Come on."

Ted followed his cousin into the hospital. They barely made it to the rest room in time. When he'd recovered, they took the elevator to the maternity ward on the fourth floor.

No sooner had they emerged than he heard Rickie's voice calling out his name. He looked up to discover his sister blocking his path.

He expected to see anger. Instead, her eyes filled with tears as she stared at the two of them.

"It's in all the newspapers and on every TV newscast. You two have done what I didn't think was possible—and you're still alive, thank God! So why aren't you happy?" She shook her head in bewilderment. "Why do you look so ill, Ted?"

His mouth was too dry from several days' sickness to moisten his lips. "Oriana had the last laugh. We thought it was the sedative Dr. Arbizu had given him that had made von Haase so unresponsive at Stroessnerplatz. We were wrong. In a few days the bad news will be all over the papers."

"What bad news?"

"The specialists in Jerusalem diagnosed him with Alzheimer's, Rickie. He's totally gone. Incompetent, incontinent. A vegetable. Unable to stand trial. We failed."

She moved closer. "How can you say that? By the very act of bringing him out of hiding, you've done a great thing for humanity. No one else could have pulled it off. You've accomplished all you can do, more than anyone would have expected or imagined. Now you both need to do something for yourselves. Get on with your lives. Get on with living and loving."

Ted felt himself cracking. "I don't think I can, Rickie."

"I don't think you can, either, not in the shape you're in. Your secret made you emotionally ill. Now it's made you physically ill, as well. Keep this up and one day soon you'll die." She gazed at him with steadfast eyes.

"So tell me—what would your death prove? Don't you think you've put your wife through enough misery already?

"I'm going to go back to the room for Ben and Miriam. Jordan will drive us home. You and Deborah need this night to yourselves.

"Bernard? Please come with me. We need to talk. As for you, my darling brother, you have a baby waiting for you in that room—and a woman who loves you. Go to her, Ted," she whispered against his cheek. "Go now."

CHAPTER FOURTEEN

THE ROOM WAS QUIET. Deborah lay on her side in the darkness. Only the light beneath the door kept it from being pitch-black. She'd fed her hungry baby. Now he was asleep in the bassinet beside her bed.

She drew it close enough to hold his tiny hand. The contact brought her enormous comfort as she listened to him make little mewling sounds.

Her other hand covered her Star of David. It brought a different kind of comfort. She pressed it against her chest, as if the weight would transport her to those days and nights of loving that would never come again.

Sooner or later Ted would show up for his duty visit, but somewhere in his mind he'd gone away from her. She knew that now. How grateful she was to Rickie who'd taken her parents home. Finally she was alone in the room to grieve over the loss of her husband.

She'd been blessed with a wonderful family and friends. Now she had a child. What mattered most was to concentrate on him, to create a happy home for the two of them.

"Deborah?"

She let out a quiet gasp. Ted had come into the room, but her thoughts had been so distant she hadn't noticed.

"Ted— I'm so happy you're back. Turn on the light so you can see the baby."

"Not yet," he whispered. "I need to talk to you. I can do it better in the dark." She felt his presence as he pulled a chair next to the bed, on the opposite side from the baby.

He can't look at our son. He's going to tell me goodbye.

Filled with fresh anxiety, she let go of the baby's hand and slowly turned to face her husband. He reached for the hand still warmed by the baby's fingers and held it between both of his.

"Rickie said you had a normal delivery, that you're fine. But I have to know the truth. Are you *really* all right?"

She heard deep concern in his voice. Her husband was an enigma to her. "Yes. I tore a little and only needed a few stitches. Dr. Lambert says I can go home in the morning."

"I'm sorry I didn't make it in time for the birth." He sounded devastated.

"It doesn't matter."

"We both know it does. You don't have to lie, Deborah. I wasn't here when you needed me most."

"You're here now. That's all I care about."

"When you hear what I have to say, it will change the way you feel about me." He let go of her hand.

She clutched at her bedsheet. "You mean you're finally going to tell me why you broke our engagement?"

"Yes. It's time."

At his admission Deborah could hardly breathe. She'd already thought of every possible scenario and had run out of explanations for his behavior. "You honestly believe I'll stop loving you after I learn the truth?"

"I know you will."

"How could anything be worse than not knowing why you broke off with me in the first place?" Deborah whispered shakily. "Why don't you just start at the beginning?"

"The beginning?"

She heard him suck in his breath.

"In the beginning my father's name was Ludwig von Haase. His father was Gerhardt von Haase—my grandfather."

In the darkness Deborah heard his words. Her body went rigid. Nothing in her life could have prepared her for this admission.

"Theodore—Ted—is the name my parents gave me to fit in with the English family tree they manufactured. Uncle John is really Uncle Valdemar, Gerhardt's firstborn son. He and my father are just a year apart.

"My grandfather smuggled his wife and children out of Alsace at the beginning of 1942. He sent them to America where he established his financial empire before he went into hiding in Paraguay.

"From his hellhole he orchestrated their lives. He saw to it that they were raised as privileged aristocrats at Graycliff, that they married girls of the best German stock, and all this under the camouflage of the Taylor name.

"Bernard's mother, Aunt Elizabeth, is the one we have to thank for leaving us a clue to our true identity. Before she died, she gave him a locket, which she hoped he'd give to his daughter one day. When he took the picture out to get it enlarged and have it framed for his grieving father, he found another picture and a note." Ted recited the note's contents.

"My Dearest Bernard,

"It's possible you will never read this. But if you do, understand that I could no longer keep still. Except for loving you with all our hearts, your father and I have lived a terrible lie.

"If you want to know our guilty secret, contact the person on the back of your father's baby picture— if she's still alive.

"I won't ask for forgiveness because there is none.

"Mother."

"On the reverse side of the photo was the name A. Duprey, Metz, France, 16/10/41. Bernard and I flew to Metz to investigate. That was the trip that turned our lives inside out.

"Andrée Duprey turned out to be the midwife

who delivered von Haase's children during the war and helped them escape. Those children were my father and Uncle John.

"The minute I learned my true identity, I realized what that knowledge would do to you and your family if you ever found out.

"Dear God, Deborah—" His voice came out on a sob. "My grandfather was responsible for the deaths of thousands of Jews—including your own grandfather and great-uncle.

"I decided a farewell letter to you was the only way to permanently sever our relationship, because I never intended to see you again.

"I've never believed in a god, but I found myself praying that if there was one, he would protect you from ever learning that you'd been sleeping with a von Haase.

"As soon as we left Metz, Bernard and I flew to Australia to tell Rickie. Her shame and guilt were as great as ours. She immediately told David good-bye and the three of us returned to New York with one thought in mind—to find our grandfather and have him brought to trial for his crimes.

"We heard he'd escaped to Paraguay. When Jordan approached Rickie for a charitable donation to fund his and Stoney's covert operation in Paraguay, we hired him to help us find von Haase.

"As you know, Rickie stowed aboard their plane. They had no choice but to take her along for the rest of the trip. While Jordan and Rickie were out on a scouting party, they came across a town in the

Chaco called Stroessnerplatz. A man turned them away from the place at gunpoint.

"When they told Father DeSilva what had happened, he said that the church had never been allowed to do missionary work there. In fact, Stroessnerplatz has been off-limits to visitors for over forty years. That information gave us our first clue that von Haase might be hiding there.

"Rickie was afraid Jordan would get killed, so she didn't want anything more to do with hunting down our grandfather. Jordan had fallen in love with her, and abided by her decision to give up the search.

"With the help of Father DeSilva, Bernard and I worked out a scheme of our own to find out if Stroessnerplatz was von Haase's stronghold. All the times I told you I was flying to England and Switzerland, Bernard and I were really making trips to Paraguay.

"Through Father DeSilva we established contact with a Dr. Arbizu. He's the personal physician of General Oriana, a military man who led a failed coup attempt against the current dictator and is preparing another.

"The doctor set up a secret meeting between us and Oriana at Stroessnerplatz, his stronghold. On a gamble, we paid the general a lot of money to help him in his takeover bid, provided he produced von Haase. The five million dollars we offered was enough bait for him to give us our grandfather.

"After the exchange, we flew that monster to Israel with a medical team and turned him over to the authorities. Unfortunately, the news leaked to the press before the doctors could confirm that von Haase has Alzheimer's disease and won't be able to stand trial."

Suddenly Deborah heard the scrape of his chair. It startled the baby who began making hungry sounds.

"The only reason I asked you to marry me again was because you were pregnant, and because I believed that if my grandfather could be tried in a war crimes court and condemned in front of your people, you might be able to forgive me enough to be able to live with me.

"But Bernard's and my plan has failed. Von Haase is a vegetable. Jews the world over will not get the satisfaction. I'm not worthy of you, Deborah. I have no right to be any child's father. As for your parents, it will be agony to behave normally around them until they leave for Jerusalem. But I'll do it for your sake.

"I know how much you must loathe and despise me, how repulsed you must be by everything I've told you. So you'll have to tell me what you want me to do.

"I'll give you a divorce whenever you say. I'll stay away from the baby and I'll never demand my rights to see him. If you want, I'll live at a hotel until your parents leave."

Her stitches hurt, making it difficult to sit up. "You're making a lot of assumptions about how I feel,'' she began quietly. Not only was there too much to absorb, her husband was so riddled with guilt, he wasn't thinking clearly right now.

"It's time for the baby's next feeding, and you're obviously exhausted. Please go to the house and try to get some sleep so you'll feel good enough to drive me home from the hospital in the morning. I'm being released at eight.''

There was a prolonged silence. "You still want me to come for you?''

"Yes. Unless you'd rather not.''

"Lord—you know that's not what I meant!''

"Didn't you ask me what I wanted?''

She heard him struggle for breath. "Yes.''

"Then believe it.''

"I'll be here at eight. Good night, Deborah.''

As soon as he'd left, she reached for the baby and put him to her breast. After she'd nursed him and he'd fallen asleep again in his bassinet, she lay there, sobbing quietly.

Not for herself.

Ted's words had finally freed her of her pain and brought her the peace she craved.

The tears she shed now were for the pain he had suffered and continued to suffer needlessly.

Many times, she and her family had talked about the guilt carried by the innocent relatives of Nazi criminals. How difficult it would be for them. But she would never have understood the depth of that guilt if she hadn't married von Haase's grandson.

Deborah thought of Ted's parents. Now she understood their agony. Their feelings of unworthiness. Their secrets, their remoteness from everyone, especially their children.

Poor Ted. Poor Rickie and Bernard. It was tragic how two generations of this family had taken on the guilt of their grandfather's crimes. He was a man who'd lived in another place, another time, when Hitler and his henchmen had gone berserk. And the Taylors were connected to him by the accident of birth.

Deborah knew how her husband's mind worked. He was an honorable man and would shrink from the knowledge that he carried von Haase blood in his veins. No wonder he couldn't acknowledge his baby.

In between visits from the nurse and more feedings, Deborah lay awake the rest of the night trying to figure out how she was going to get through to her husband. He needed to know she loved him, that she didn't blame him for his grandfather's evil.

How would she convince him that her parents loved him, too? When they learned the truth, nothing would change. Like Deborah, they would love him and Bernard even more for risking their lives to search for justice.

She pondered her dilemma until morning. By then she had a plan, but she was going to need her parents' help.

ALL DAY, Ted felt like he'd been walking on the edge of a precipice. Since he'd picked up Deborah and the baby from the hospital, she'd been loving and gentle with him. Her behavior was completely normal—almost, he thought, as if she'd forgotten what he'd told her. Once home, Miriam had taken over the baby's care, leaving Ted free to be with Benjamin while Deborah slept on and off.

When he went to their bedroom to see if he could bring her something to eat or drink, she told him she was craving Chinese food. Would he mind driving clear across town to bring her some takeout from a place she particularly liked?

Surprised at the request, he did her bidding. In truth, he was glad to escape the house for an hour.

Since last night when he'd told her the truth, he'd felt as if he were sitting on a time bomb, waiting for it to go off. They *had* to talk about this. But Deborah hadn't given him an opening. He hated pressuring her on her first day home from the hospital, but he couldn't go another night without their situation being resolved.

Finally it was time for bed. With a sense of urgency he said good-night to her parents and headed for the master bedroom. Deborah had been silent long enough. They needed to talk. Now.

To his chagrin, she was asleep when he entered the room. So was the baby, who slept in the cradle by her side of the bed. Upset because any conversation would have to be put off until later, he jerked off his clothes and slid under the covers. He was careful to make sure their bodies didn't touch.

Ten minutes later his anxiety set off an adrenaline

attack. He got out of the bed, threw on his robe and began pacing. The baby began to cry.

That was good. Deborah would have to feed him and then he'd ask her what she had decided to do about their marriage, about him.

"Darling?" she murmured sleepily. "I'm too tired. Would you carry the baby into Mom's room? She said she'd give him some formula the hospital sent home. There are several bottles in the fridge. Just warm one of them for a minute or two, will you?"

He swallowed hard. "Of course. Go back to sleep."

"Thank you."

So far she hadn't asked him to deal with the baby. He couldn't refuse. There was no choice but to take the baby to Miriam.

Flicking on the bedside light so he could see where he was going, he went around to the cradle. After lifting the baby in his arms, he held it against his shoulder so he wouldn't have to look at it.

The baby cried harder than ever, obviously because his mother wasn't the one holding him. By the time Ted reached the door to his in-laws' room, both Miriam and Ben were up. It reminded him of the time he'd awakened Deborah's father at the hotel on the eve of their wedding.

"Let's all go downstairs and feed the baby. Deborah needs her rest," her father suggested.

Since neither of them offered to take the baby from Ted, it would be churlish to ask one of them to relieve him. Once they reached the kitchen, Miriam would take over and Ted could go back upstairs. Tired though Deborah was, he would force her to talk to him. He couldn't stand this nightmare any longer.

Ben beat him to the refrigerator and brought out one of the bottles to warm in a cup of hot water. By now the baby seemed inconsolable.

"Miriam?"

She smiled. "Don't panic. Sit down and relax. I think that bottle's about ready, don't you, Ben?"

He nodded and first tested the warmth of the bottle's contents on his inner wrist, then handed it to Ted. Ted could see no alternative; he took it and put the nipple in the baby's mouth. For the first time he had to actually look at his son.

The baby was dressed in a pale blue nightie, tied at the neck.

He had midnight blue eyes and a dusting of dark hair like Deborah's. His features looked so tiny and perfect. Yet his body was strong and long. So were his fingers, which were squared at the ends.

Like mine. Except for his coloring, he's a von Haase.

At first the baby didn't like the bottle.

"Maybe you'd better do this, Miriam."

"No, no. You're doing fine," she said as the baby finally stopped fighting him and settled down to drink.

Ben nodded. "He's a lucky little boy to have a father like you."

"How many children will be able to tell *their* children that their father risked his life to bring a Nazi war criminal to justice? Eh?"

Ted froze in the chair.

"That's right, Miriam. How many children will be able to brag that their father was a hero to millions and millions of people who've wondered where von Haase went when he escaped so many years ago?"

"I know how I feel." Miriam's voice shook. She put her arms around Ted's shoulders from behind and kissed the top of his head.

"You have done something for me that no one else could. Because of you, I know that von Haase didn't escape to a life of luxury.

"Because of you and your courageous cousin, we now know that he was forced to live the rest of his life in exile without his family. In destroying lives, he destroyed his own. And he lived long enough to be dying of Alzheimer's disease—which in some ways is the ultimate destruction of a life.

"He couldn't have enjoyed those years in the Paraguayan jungle, living with other criminals. No doubt his nights were long, and his dreams were haunted by the crimes he committed. I couldn't wish a better penance for him. Thank you for this priceless gift, Ted. Ben and I have loved you from the moment we met. Now there are millions who love you, too, even if they don't know your name."

"Like I told you at the wedding," Ben interjected, "you were the man I wanted for my daughter. What you've done for the Jewish people, what you continue to do for us, has only intensified those feelings. I'm proud to be your father-in-law.''

"Ted…" Miriam said softly. "There's someone upstairs who loves you more than you know. Go on. We'll take care of your son for the rest of the night.''

"While you're at it," Ben added, "will you two decide on a name? We don't know what to call our grandson. I think he's beginning to wonder what's wrong with everybody.''

Ted was too choked up to talk. Miriam took the baby from his arms. The second he stood up, the two men embraced for a long moment. Then he ran from the kitchen, taking the stairs two at a time.

But when he reached the second floor and opened the door to their bedroom, he hesitated, fearing this might all be a dream with no substance.

"Come here, Ted. I've been waiting for you.''

The love in her voice drew him to her side. When he lay down next to her, she pulled him close.

It could have been a half hour they stayed like that, rocking back and forth while she buried her face in his hair and gave him her love. Every bit of it.

"I don't know how you can forgive me,'' he finally muttered. "After what you and I shared in Jerusalem; after what your parents taught me at the Holocaust memorial—to find out I was a von Haase… Oh, God, Deborah—''

His voice cracked, then he broke into deep, wracking sobs.

"Shh." She hugged him harder, murmuring endearments. "If it's possible, I love you more for what you've told me. So do my parents. But your suffering has been too great."

She put her hand under his chin and lifted it, then bent her head to kiss the mouth he'd been hiding from her.

At first he was unresponsive, but she was fighting for her life. For their lives. Slowly she was able to coax an answering kiss from him.

When he suddenly deepened their kiss, her heart leapt in her chest. Love seemed to pour from his very soul. She felt his tears on her face.

"I love you, I worship you, Deborah. I don't understand how you can love me knowing who I am."

"You're Ted Taylor, the man I fell in love with. I don't care about some maniac ancestor of yours who lived and functioned in a totally different world half a century ago. It doesn't matter because he has nothing to do with you and me, or our baby."

"The baby—he's wonderful, Deborah."

"I think so, too."

"Forgive me for not being here for you when you needed me."

"You had pressing business in Paraguay. Who else on this earth had more reason or right to find von Haase than his own grandchildren? One day soon I want to hear every detail. But right now I just want to hold you for the rest of the night."

"I'm afraid, darling."

"Of what?"

"What if I'm not a good father?"

"What if I'm not a good mother?"

"Don't be ridiculous."

Deborah chuckled at his swift defense of her. "I was just going to say the same thing to you. We'll learn together."

He kissed her thoroughly, still unable to believe the nightmare was finally over.

"We need to think of a name for our son."

"I know," he whispered. "Your father reminded me before I came upstairs."

"I thought we'd name him after our fathers. After all, if it wasn't for them giving us life, you and I wouldn't be here." Her voice caught on the words. "Can you imagine not knowing the wonder of a love like ours?"

"BENJAMIN ALEXANDER SOLOMON TAYLOR. That is such a nice name, a good name." Rickie imitated Deborah's Aunt Essie to perfection.

Deborah laughed and hugged Rickie as they stood with arms around each other's waists in the middle of Deborah's crowded living room. The women's talk centered on the baby.

"Did you notice he didn't cry once during the ceremony?"

"He was perfect, just like our Sol."

"I think he has the shape of Deborah's eyes."

"What about their color?"

"Right now they're blue. It could go either way. Lena's didn't turn brown for a year."

"He'll be tall like his handsome father."

"And dark!"

"His mouth curls just like Deborah's did when she was born."

"When he pouts, he reminds me of David."

Surrounded by loving family and friends who'd just witnessed the Brith Milah and baby-naming ceremony, Deborah thought the cacophony of voices and conversation was the sweetest music she'd ever heard.

And watching Ted and Bernard at their fathers' sides, the four of them chatting amiably with Deborah's father and brother, was perhaps the sweetest sight she'd ever seen. Except for one night in their bedroom, when Ted examined his son for the first time and discovered how much he loved him.

Her gaze drifted to Jordan and Stoney, who were having a private discussion with Father DeSilva. In the short time since Deborah had been home from the hospital, everyone in both families had learned the truth about everything.

Deborah was very much aware of the vital role this remarkable priest had played in the operation to locate Ted's grandfather, and the role he continued to play in Jordan's and Rickie's lives. So many good people had taken serious risks in the name of honor and decency.

Laughter in another corner caught Deborah's attention, and she glanced at Mary. Though Jordan and Rickie were official godparents to little Ben, Deborah had asked Mary to be an honorary godmother.

The older woman had never had children of her own, and she seemed overjoyed. Somehow she'd wrested the baby from Ted. Now, followed by Michelle, Stoney's soon-to-be-wife for the second time, Mary was parading him in front of the guests and refused to relinquish her hold of him, much to the chagrin of Deborah's aunts, who had yet to play with him as long as they wanted.

Her uncles were having their usual philosophical discussion with anyone who would listen—in this case Rabbi Arnavitz.

As her gaze traveled from one face to another, she heard her mother call to her and Rickie from the couch where she was seated with Ted's mother. To her delight, the two seemed to be enjoying each other's company.

"Will you look at the present they've given your son, Deborah?" Her mom lifted the Noah's Ark mezuzah for everyone to see.

"It's lovely," Deborah murmured. "Thank you for such a thoughtful gift."

"You'll have to get Ted to put it up on the door frame of the nursery."

"I heard that, Miriam."

Ted seemed to have materialized out of thin air. He slid his arms around Deborah's waist from behind.

The desire to melt against her husband was a

temptation at any time, but never more so than since the baby was born. Dr. Lambert had warned them both against making love too soon.

He nestled Deborah closer. The gesture was so sensual, she couldn't quite catch her breath. "I think we'll go upstairs and do it right now." The double entendre brought a red flush to her cheeks, as it was supposed to. She turned and buried her face against his shoulder. Their desire for each other was growing out of control.

"Excuse us," he muttered to no one in particular. With the gift in one hand and his other arm around her shoulders, he ushered her to the foyer and up the staircase.

"We'll bypass the nursery, I think."

"No— Ted! We can't…" she cried half in alarm, half in excitement, as he swept her into the master bedroom.

"Explain what that word means, darling." He put the gift on a side table before forcing Deborah to walk backward until she fell onto the bed. The blaze of desire turned his eyes a hot blue as he followed her down.

"But—"

"Little Ben's not in there to separate us anymore—or to interrupt us."

His narrowed gaze studied the shape of her face, her mouth, then fell lower. "Do you know how I can tell how many times your heart beats a minute?

She shook her head, overwhelmed by the feelings he could arouse in her.

"The diamonds in your pendant catch the light with each beat and flicker. I can count them. One, two, three, four, five, six— They're flickering too fast for me to keep up."

Her low laughter was smothered by his mouth. He kissed her playfully, he kissed her passionately. "You've made me happier than any man has a right to be. You know that, don't you?" he whispered with tears in his voice.

Deborah started to tell him what he meant to her, but the sound of her mother's voice broke through the wave of her euphoria.

"Hello? Ted? Deborah? Where are you? Ben's fussing and needs his mother. Everybody's coming upstairs to peek in the nursery and see how the mezuzah looks on the door. The rabbi wants to say goodbye. The caterer would like to know where you put the rest of the champagne. Your fath—"

"Just a minute, Mom," an embarrassed Deborah called out. "We'll be right there."

"Just kidding," Miriam said through the door.

Ted let out a bark of laughter.

"I'm glad to see both of you using the good brains you were born with. Your father and I aren't getting any younger. He told me to remind you there are more family names waiting to be given. The sooner the better."

Ted's shoulders shook while he tried to contain his laughter. Deborah was having the same trouble. He pulled her on top of him. They stared into each other's eyes. The laughter subsided. He unfastened her hair, and it fell all around them in rich, warm-brown waves.

"I have a present for you."

"No, darling. No more presents. You've done too much already."

"This is a different kind of present. I've memorized a poem for you on our son's special day."

"A poem?" Her eyes closed. This man she'd married. She loved him so much.

"It's called *The First Princess (to Nechama)*. I came across it recently. A woman named Mina Friedler wrote it.

"It spoke to me. It says everything I want to say to you, but says it so beautifully."

"I want to hear it," she begged.

He traced the shape of her face with his finger, then began.

"When Miriam took Benjamin,

"He gave me you.

"Your saucer eyes drink the first few months of life. Your regal form kicks on a snow white blanket.

"A child of Zion in blue velvet cries as if you call to all generations.

"Out of your little lungs comes Sarah's laughter, Rachel's joy, Leah's tears caressing down my cheek.

"In time your velvet dress becomes too small, the snow white blanket fades.

"You grow into your years, walk with your
father's eyes, your mother's pride.
"Bend before the Torah's commandments.
"Bring inside the Shabbos light,
"And now you stand a woman of Zion.
"My wife."

He rested his head against her heaving breast.
"You're my life, Deborah. I swear I'll love you till
the day I die."

HARLEQUIN SUPERROMANCE®

DEBORAH'S SON

by award-winning author
Rebecca Winters

Deborah's pregnant. The man she loves—the baby's
father—doesn't know. He's withdrawn from her for reasons
she doesn't understand. But she has to tell him. *Wants* to tell
him. She wants them to be a family.

Available in October
wherever Harlequin books are sold.

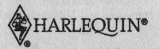

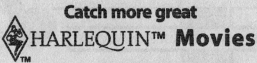

HARLEQUIN SUPERROMANCE®

HOME ON THE RANCH

BUFFALO GAL

by Lisa McAllister

**Welcome to White Thunder Ranch
in North Dakota!**

Andrea Moore learns on her wedding day that she's won a buffalo ranch. In less than twenty-four hours, Andrea's life changes completely. It goes from predictable to surprising...and exciting. Especially when she meets White Thunder's foreman, Mike Winterhawk—who's determined to protect his business from a city woman who knows squat about ranching!

Watch for *Buffalo Gal* in November 1998.
Available wherever Harlequin books are sold.

HARLEQUIN®

Makes any time special ™

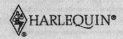

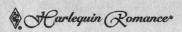

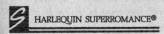

HARLEQUIN SUPERROMANCE®

FINDERS, KEEPERS

Is a detective agency that specializes in finding lost loves, friends, family, etc...

If Noah had been adventurous enough to discover the world and himself, he could be adventurous enough to visit an agency that specialized in finding lost lovers. But meeting Maggie Tyrell, proprietor, was an adventure in itself. However, Maggie wouldn't be deterred from the task at hand—even if Noah wanted her to call off the search. *Even if it meant her heart would break...*

Found: One Wife

Harlequin Superromance (#809)
October 1998

by Judith Arnold

Available wherever Harlequin books are sold.

❖ HARLEQUIN®

COMING NEXT MONTH

#810 BUFFALO GAL • Lisa McAllister
Home on the Ranch
When Dr. Andrea Moore awakes on her wedding day, the last
thing she expects is to end up—still single—stranded with a
rock band on her new buffalo ranch in North Dakota. True,
she is a vet, but a *buffalo* vet? More surprising still is her
attraction to the foreman, Mike Winterhawk. He wants her
ranch, and she seems to want…*him!*

#811 BEFORE THANKSGIVING COMES • Marisa Carroll
Family Man
Widower Jake Walthers is a hardworking man who's busy
taking care of his three young children. He doesn't have time
for anything else—certainly not love. Then an accident leaves
him in need of help, and his neighbor Allison Martin is the
only one he can turn to. He doesn't mean to fall for Allison—
she's too "big city" for his liking—but when he does, he
learns she has her own reasons for not getting involved….

#812 IT HAPPENED IN TEXAS • Darlene Graham
Guaranteed Page-Turner
Every morning since her husband's death, Marie Manning
wakes up and reassures herself that her children are fine
and her home is secure. But her world goes from safe to
scary when a neighbor makes a grisly discovery on Marie's
ranch. It doesn't help that Sheriff Jim Whittington thinks
Marie knows more than she's telling. And it *certainly* doesn't
help that her heart beats a little faster every time the sheriff
comes over.

#813 JULIA • Shannon Waverly
Circle of Friends
They'd been friends growing up, living on the small East
Coast island called Harmony. Now one of them is dead,
and Julia Lewis goes home for the first time in seven
years. To a funeral… But coming home is also a chance
to reconnect with her circle of old friends—and to meet
a new man, Ben Grant. A man who causes complications
in Harmony's world…and in Julia's.